the girl and the rat

ALSO BY JARI JÄRVELÄ

The Girl and the Bomb

the girl and the rat

JARI JÄRVELÄ

Translated by Kristian London

amazoncrossing

Text copyright © 2015 Jari Järvelä
Translation copyright © 2016 Kristian London
All rights reserved.

Previously published as *Tyttö ja rotta* by Tammi Publishers in Finland in 2015. Translated from Finnish by Kristian London. First published in English by AmazonCrossing in 2016.

Published by AmazonCrossing, Seattle

www.apub.com

Amazon, the Amazon logo, and AmazonCrossing are trademarks of Amazon.com, Inc., or its affiliates.

ISBN-13: 9781503953871
ISBN-10: 1503953874

Cover design by Christopher Salyers

Printed in the United States of America

"Imagine a city where graffiti wasn't illegal . . . and stop leaning against the wall—it's wet."

—*Banksy*

I: THE ICE RATS

1: THE ICE RATS

MINUS 24 HOURS

I was riding in a clanking S-Bahn with my four best friends—my only friends. There's no way I could have guessed that within twenty-four hours two of us would be dead and a third one would be laid out, leg totally jacked.

And that third one would be me.

We were about to burn the train; that was the reason we had split up and staked out different spots around the car, which reeked of garlic. Verboten indicated we had two more stations. He was the only one standing.

Night was turning to day.

Verboten carried a raincoat over his arm. He was leaning against the end of the car so we all had a clear view of him the whole time. His job was to give the signal at the crucial moment.

He was reading a book. He would occasionally look up when the train lurched, check to see what the next stop was, and then turn the page with a lick of his finger.

An astute observer would have wondered about a couple of things going on here. First: Why was the ugly guy with the red face lugging around a raincoat on a summer morning forecast to be mostly sunny and the start of a new heat wave? Second: How was he able to read the book he was holding when it was upside down?

Plus: Why were five passengers wearing *shemaghs*, Palestinian scarves, around their necks?

Verboten had forgotten his eyeglasses at home; he was nervous. This stretch of track was new, and burning a train when it's light outside is a totally different thing from doing it at night. This was our first daytime gig. An extremely necessary one, Verboten had stressed. We needed to record our work in daylight. That's why this time we, the children of the night, hadn't left our lair until dawn.

Verboten was using the raincoat as a screen. Underneath the rustling fabric he was hiding a spike-tipped stonemason's hammer.

The second he had stepped into the car he had slapped a black sticker across the lens of the surveillance camera with a thumb-press faster than a right jab from Klitschko.

All of us carried black stickers in every pocket of every pair of pants we owned. In our profession, they were as necessary as the wrenches in a mechanic's toolbox.

I scanned the innocent people sitting around us. They didn't have a clue as to what was about to happen.

The couple sitting across from me was arguing so violently their bench was shaking. The woman had a long face and hair that reached down to her shoulders; she had just announced she was going to shave it all off. The guy protested furiously, demanding she grow it down to the small of her back. The quarrel had continued until they were glaring at each other as coldly as flatfish frozen under the ice. They sat there, taking turns showing the right length, as if they were calibrating the official measure of a meter.

A sunken-cheeked sixty-year-old was perched next to me; his legs were so short they swung a couple of inches off the floor. A black-and-white feather adorned his brimless moss-green cap, the kind

Robin Hood must have sported when he romped around Sherwood Forest. But instead of loosing arrows carved from yew wood, Sunken Cheeks was pelleting the floor with the projectiles he was digging out of his nose.

How would his obituary describe him if the train went off the rails? *The man who spent his final moments firing snot balls.*

The train slowed as it pulled into the station. No one got off, but a woman pushing a stroller got on.

Bad choice, this train car. Life was full of them. We berate ourselves for our bad choices, but we make the lousiest ones without even realizing they're mistakes.

Verboten moved aside to make room for her, shifted to the steel pole running from floor to ceiling.

And then, just before the sliding doors closed, a policewoman strode into the car. She yawned and took a seat across the aisle from me. I had a cloth bag between my ankles; instinctively, I clamped it even tighter between my feet.

I looked over at Verboten, but he was concentrating on his upside-down paperback.

The train picked up speed; the walls of apartment buildings flashed past. When I squinted, the still-burning streetlamps formed an unbroken string of pearls.

Vorkuta was sitting two rows away from me; Alyosha was pretending to snooze. Both looked at Verboten from behind the policewoman's back and shook their heads.

Verboten acted like he didn't notice. As he turned the page of his book he left his forefinger raised a moment longer than necessary. One more station.

The train was half-empty; the commuters were still brushing their teeth and popping their blackheads in front of their mirrors.

The policewoman yawned and checked the route map above her head as sourly as if it were a letter from the tax collector. She carried a pistol at her hip; the leather holster was worn at the edges, as if she'd had plenty of practice drawing it.

The train stopped again. I clenched my fists until my knuckles turned white, which was the closest I ever came to praying. I wished the policewoman would jump off.

Instead, she pulled her blond hair back into a ponytail and stayed put. Even worse, another police officer walked onto the train, a guy. He went over to chat with his colleague.

I tried to catch Verboten's attention by making a face. He had closed his book and was reverently studying the back cover, as if he might find undiscovered lines to the Lord's Prayer there. He had transferred the raincoat to his armpit.

I was sweating like I was in the Sahara, despite the fact that the station's ventilation ducts were thrumming. Cool, coal-laden air from the tunnels was blowing in through the train's cracked-open windows. The fake leather seat under my butt was soaking.

The instant the train pulled out of the station, Vorkuta stood and walked down the aisle toward Verboten. They conversed in low hisses, and their disagreement ended with Verboten yanking the emergency brake. Even though I'd been prepared for a sudden stop, it came so unexpectedly that I flew face-first into the laps of the bickering couple sitting across from me. The guy had just taken hold of his girlfriend's hair, and he tore out a hunk as he pitched forward. That resolved the argument.

Both cops flew. The male cop bashed his head against the steel pole; he was on his knees, holding his temples.

By the time I was stumbling up the aisle, Verboten had wrenched open the sliding doors. I was the last one out; even Smew had slipped past me. Meanwhile, Verboten was pounding steel stakes under the doors, leaving a gap the width of a fist between them. As long as the stakes jammed the doors it would be impossible to open or close them.

Verboten raced to the next pair of doors, pounding stakes into the spaces between them so they couldn't be forced open from the inside.

Smew was videorecording the whole time.

"Shemagh," he said. I drew my scarf up over my nose and wrapped it around my head; the only visible part of my face was a horizontal crack through which I watched everything. I pulled on a pair of surgical gloves.

As long as a single pair of doors was open, the train's automatic warning system would prevent it from moving.

The train had four cars. I was responsible for bombing two sides; Alyosha and Vorkuta were going to paint the rest of the train. Verboten's job was to stop people from coming out. Smew's was to film the operation.

I started from the car I'd been riding in. I sprayed an electric-blue zigzag and white blotch of snow, then in black, right in the middle, quickly dashed out ICE RATS.

I wrote across the windows in white-hot tints, blanketing the faces staring out. Someone inside was using their phone to record me.

I adjusted my scarf and finished dressing up the glass.

The policewoman was pounding on the window from the inside. She yelled at me to stop. She could yell all she wanted.

"Two minutes!" Verboten shouted.

It normally took the guards five minutes to show up. That meant we needed to paint in four.

I chucked the empty can to the tracks. I didn't have time to check the rest of the crew's progress. As I whipped out a fresh can of blue, my other hand was spraying white; I was bombing with two hands at the same time.

The train was gradually transforming into a huge chunk of ice.

As I painted the final windows, someone grabbed my shoulder. The policewoman had slipped her hand through the gap in the doors. Her grip was like a pair of tongs.

"You're under arrest," she said.

I pressed the nozzle on my can of spray paint and turned her face ice blue. She let go and blindly groped for the pistol at her hip.

"One minute!" Verboten shouted.

I started in on another can.

Painting with a fire extinguisher would have been faster, but the result wouldn't have been as clean. Plus, it would have been impossible to carry extinguishers filled with paint onto the trains without security guards or police officers interfering.

"Guards in view," Vorkuta shouted, bolting up from the last car.

The uniforms were running up the track from the station. They had a German shepherd with them; it strained at its leash and bared its teeth like Cerberus, the guard dog of Hell.

I'm afraid of dogs. One bit me when I was a kid. The only thing its owner worried about was whether her manicured man-eater's show-quality teeth had been ruined by sinking into a black girl's flesh.

"Go, go, go, go!" Verboten shouted. Smew pulled up last of all, filming the approaching guards. His final shot was a long panorama of the burned train. It wasn't a red-and-brown S-Bahn anymore; it was an icicle that had mysteriously appeared in Berlin's urban landscape, glittering in the pale morning light like an Arctic snowfield.

I ran past the conductor's cab. Alyosha had dressed up the window, spraying a pointy-nosed rat's face where the driver's face should have been.

"Ice Rats forrrrrrever," he yelped.

The German shepherd barked; the guards behind us roared at us to halt.

Sprinting down the track toward the bridge, I was aware of the buttoned-up half zombies stepping out of the corner cafes, coffee cups in hand. Sleepy, slow, heavy jowled, weighed down by everyday concerns, dead to life's pulse, its rush.

Verboten pulled up next to me. "Don't drift so close to the middle. That's where the electricity is," he panted, before flying past me.

Verboten was the one who'd planned our escape routes. He had trained as an electrician and understood precisely where we could and couldn't step. His advance across the middle of the bridge looked like that old video game where you crossed the river by jumping from rock to rock, trying not to fall in while a gorilla hurled boulders at your head.

The guards had stopped at the end of the bridge. They were too afraid of getting electrocuted.

Just the previous week, on a night like this, they had unleashed one of their German shepherds, and the poor pooch fried to death. Its ferocious barks had ended in a pop and a sizzle.

We crossed the tracks to the other side of the river, where we climbed down a narrow ladder welded to a steel post. We wove through a maze of warehouses and hopped on a passing tram. We had pulled the shemaghs from our heads and shoved them in our pockets.

"Your face is red," Alyosha said. "Are you scared?"

"You're pale as shit," I retorted. "Are you scared?"

"I'm always pale," he muttered.

We got off at the end of the line and walked about ten minutes, until we reached a building that was missing most of one side. The gaping fire wall made it look like the structure was shouting. Through the huge hole, you could see a toilet and the pipe leading from it; the pipe ended in midair.

It had been a while since the first swing of the wrecking ball. Just as the bulldozers dug in, two briefcase-wielding men delivered a cease and desist order. Verboten had managed to finagle a temporary injunction by claiming that rare artifacts from late in the tenth century had been discovered in the basement, predating current estimates of Berlin's founding by over two hundred years. An archaeological dig was necessary. The demolition had been called off and two-thirds of the building remained standing as the case crawled through the courts.

The only reminder of the plans for the site was the sign erected in the empty lot behind it: a picture of a glass office cube and the words IMAGINE YOUR COMPANY HERE! An old warehouse stood on the other side of our building; many of its small windows were shattered, thanks to the rocks that had been chucked through the panes. The cracks in its brick walls were full of swifts' nests. There was no activity in this warehouse to speak of, if you didn't count the birds.

Our building had been declared uninhabitable because the water had been cut off and the electricity worked only intermittently. The building's attic, or the part that still remained, was our realm. A rotating cast of vagabonds occupied some of the empty apartments on the lower floors. The second story was exclusively vacated office space; all that was left of the big dreams that had once flourished there were the brass plates next to the doors. The padding from the mattresses at the Little Heaven massage company provided housing for a thriving mouse colony. A constant, shrill whine chittered from the depths of the stuffing.

The upper stories had borne the brunt of the interrupted demolition.

The lock on the building's front door was busted. A steel post stood on either side of it; entry was prevented by sturdy plastic orange mesh drawn between them.

Boards had been pounded across the stairs to bar access to the upper floors; a bilingual sign had been nailed to them: VERBOTEN! ACHTUNG! FORBIDDEN! DANGER!

That's where Verboten got his name.

MINUS 19 HOURS

I was lying on my lumpy mattress. Smew had glued himself next to Alyosha at the computers. We had two desktops; Verboten had snagged old-school monitors and hardware from the Dumpsters of companies upgrading their equipment. There were also a couple of cardboard boxes full of stuff pilfered in the same fashion: motherboards, hard drives, memory cards, and handfuls of spare parts that clever fingers could put to use.

Our desk was a door laid across legs of stacked bricks; the handle still poked up between the monitors. Smew and Alyosha had wound the cables around it to keep them from drifting across the table. A weeping lioness pierced by arrows had been painted on one of the door's wooden panels.

The lioness had been there before our arrival in Berlin. In her honor Smew and Alyosha named their workspace Lion Killer. I had asked what the hell the name had to do with anything. Alyosha had explained that the world wasn't a democracy; it was a plutocracy where power was concentrated among the very rich. The predator was the world, sickened by its lust for power and money, and they shot healing arrows at her in video form.

I went over and scratched the lioness by her whiskers, watching as the counter ratcheted up numbers: 57,000 views.

Smew had edited the video during our tram ride. As soon as we'd made it to the attic he uploaded it to YouTube.

Our four-person crew had arrived in Berlin six weeks ago: me, Smew, Alyosha, and Vorkuta.

We'd been squatting for weeks in the deserted city of Pripyat, Ukraine, right next to the Chernobyl nuclear power plant. The city had been proclaimed uninhabitable: ABSOLUTELY NO TRESPASSING ALLOWED. We had inhabited it, no problem.

In Pripyat I had created a piece in Rust's memory, Smew had photographed the desolation, and Alyosha and Vorkuta had done their own thing. The two of them had been to Pripyat on numerous occasions. We ate mushrooms they picked and hares they snared and fish they trapped. A couple of times Vorkuta offered me rat steak; I passed and had to live with my growling, cramping stomach. Some nights, it felt like I was ticking, even without my radiation gauge.

I had followed Smew into one of Pripyat's abandoned homes and browsed through a newspaper almost thirty years old. It had been left open on the table during the occupants' rushed departure. In one yellowed photograph a soccer goalie was throwing himself into the air to block a kick. Did it go into the net or not? I had no idea. I couldn't read the Cyrillic letters.

The days grew longer as I painted. After I finished all three walls of my piece, I spent most of my time lying up on the roof, watching the swallows. Birch trees grew out of cracks in the roof; the tallest were over ten meters. The concrete shell that had been built around the destroyed reactor loomed at the edge of Pripyat, like a whale rising from the sea.

Then Vorkuta announced we had to cut out. Soldiers were headed to Pripyat to conduct a sweep of the city. There was no doubting the accuracy of the information, and anyone they found would be facing jail time or the barrel of a gun. We bailed as abruptly as the previous inhabitants did under threat of nuclear radiation. We left most of our stuff behind.

Smew had suggested Berlin. Verboten was an old buddy of his and always had "some interesting new project" going on.

We didn't really have a choice. Vorkuta was pacing restlessly in circles; Alyosha had parked himself on the roof, in my former sunbathing spot, to scan the horizon.

We arrived at Berlin Hauptbahnhof at night. The convoluted journey from Pripyat had lasted four days; we started the last leg in Warsaw. Our train car had suffered a locked wheel at the very end of the trip, and we had sent sparks flying as we entered Berlin through its eastern suburbs.

Smew had called Verboten from the station in Warsaw and scrawled his address on a scrap of paper. It had taken us half the night to make our way to the crumbling apartment building where Verboten lived. A sense of scale wasn't Smew's strong suit. After checking a map, he had determined it was only a couple hundred yards to our destination. By the time we got there, our feet told us we had run a marathon. Under a streetlamp, Alyosha showed us the blisters he'd gotten during our three-hour hike, while moths whirred in the halo of light.

Pillheads roamed the street outside Verboten's building; most of them had a hard time staying on their feet, but they still demanded money from us. One of them waved a dirty needle and threatened to infect every single one of us with AIDS if we didn't open up our wallets.

We managed to push our way past them and up the stairs. Needle Jabber staggered after us. He kept shouting that we were trespassing. If we didn't leave right away he was going to beat us to death. It was his right, he was just protecting his home.

We had just met one of our new neighbors. What a pleasure.

Verboten was waiting for us on the second-floor landing; we could still hear Needle Jabber's yammering. Our host was one scary-looking dude. The left side of his face was badly burnt, and the creased skin on that half blazed an angry red, as if he were always blushing. His left eyelid drooped down; it never pulled up all the way. It made him look like he was always napping.

But Verboten wasn't blushing or asleep. Plus he had this raspy way of breathing that reminded me of Darth Vader.

He led us through a labyrinth of corridors and staircases; we were climbing the whole time. He told the guys to go up the final staircase, open the door, and then crawl carefully to the right. But he stopped me in my tracks. He said he didn't know me, and he wasn't in the habit of letting anyone he didn't know into his home.

He wanted to know something about me. Smew had warned me to skip the bands I liked and my favorite colors and get straight to the point. I cleared my throat and said that I had killed two people.

I glanced around at all the rebar piercing the concrete. The building was on the verge of ruin. I was standing on disintegrating stairs. The treads had collapsed in places, leaving behind half stairs with a black chasm underneath. Boards had been placed across this semistaircase, along with a red-and-yellow caution tape.

VERBOTEN! DANGER!

Verboten was sitting on the other side of the tape, swinging his feet in the void left by a missing step.

In Kotka, back in Finland, I had lived in the ghetto of Karhuvuori, where almost half the residents were unemployed. At first I lived there with Mom, then with Rust. My apartment had been in a yellow building where the walls were so poorly insulated you could hear the couple on one side fighting and the budding guitarist on the other side practicing for *Star Search*. And this was at four in the morning. But it was rarely a problem. At that time, I was either out painting graffiti or delivering the morning mail.

Compared to Verboten's apartment building, my home in Karhuvuori was a palace; at least in Karhuvuori all the building's external walls were still standing. This building was missing an entire side, and the wrecking ball had smashed away parts of the adjoining exterior walls, so when you opened a door you didn't know if you'd step into an apartment or plummet ten meters to the ground. Some of the stairs and walls had been sledgehammered.

The elevator shaft at my side yawned; the doors to the shaft were open but there was no sign of the elevator itself. Snapped cables swung slowly, rocked by the air currents traveling through the shaft.

"Tell me about your family," Verboten said to the silence. "Did you kill them, too?"

"My mom lives in Finland, in Kotka. She reads tarot cards over the phone for gullible idiots. Or else she bottles tap water, adds a few drops of food coloring and a pinch of oregano, and claims the bottle contains an elixir that will cure cancer. She even believes it herself. I haven't heard anything from my dad since he ran away from Finland. He got called a nigger one too many times. He was a coward for running."

"You ran away, too," Verboten said. "Went and hid in the shadows of a nuclear power plant."

I could feel the stare through his drooping eyelid.

"Yeah, I ran away."

"That makes you a coward, too."

"Why the fuck are you giving me such a hard time? I didn't come to a shithole like this to listen to your BS. I came because Smew asked me to. I trust him. I don't know you from Adam. I haven't eaten in four days. I've been traveling in nasty trains that reek of garlic and feet. My legs are numb and my back aches. Even when you change trains, you end up surrounded by the stench of garlic and feet and piss. It's probably some cleaning product they use. And you know what? Compared to your place those trains feel like six-star hotels."

The corner of Verboten's mouth twitched; his face was so fire-scarred that it was impossible to tell what the twitch meant.

He stood up. It was only now that I noticed he had an old sword in one hand. Verboten raised the sword and lowered its blade, flat side down, on each of my shoulders.

"Metro, I name you knight of the fortress of the Ice Rats. You must never reveal the location of this fortress to anyone, and you must defend it from all intruders and enemy assaults to the death."

"News flash. This is an apartment building," I retorted. "A shithole that's on the verge of collapsing."

Verboten didn't answer. He walked up the hole-ridden stairs and stopped at a door. The same kind of red-and-yellow tape was drawn across it as was drawn across the staircase down below.

VERBOTEN! ACHTUNG! VERBOTEN!

"I see your name is on the door," I said. "Do you get a lot of mail? Is Achtung your first name? Whose idea was it to name you that, Achtung Verboten? Your mom's or your dad's?"

I should have kept my mouth shut, but Verboten had riled me up. He didn't answer.

There was a bolt across the door, and Verboten wrestled it open.

"Turn to the right when you come in," Verboten said. "If you come in."

Verboten left the door cracked behind him. I hesitated for a moment, and then I strode after him on my long legs.

And almost dropped into emptiness.

There was no floor.

MINUS 16 HOURS

I was gnawing on a sandwich; the lettuce looked like it had been run over by a truck. My plate was covered in the same black specks as the lettuce. When I poked at them, one started to move.

Someone had smeared greasy palmprints on the window next to my head. They turned the sunny street outside into a pea-soup fog.

I was sitting in a bar a few blocks from the Ice Cave, eating breakfast. It was already noon. No one else from the Ice Cave had felt like coming with me, so I asked for three cups of coffee to go.

I headed back past the warehouse and stopped when I got to our apartment building. The sun was warming the stucco; I leaned against the wall for a moment to bask in its heat like a lizard. A tiny black ant crossed from the wall to my wrist on an exploratory expedition; its legs tickled.

"Where can a guy get some coffee around here?"

I squinted. A white van had pulled up. The window was down; a jacketed elbow was poking out. I tried to see into the van, but the sun was shining in my eyes.

I swung the paper bag in the direction of the bar.

"How much?" the elbow asked.

"I'm sure you can afford it."

"How much to get laid?"

"What?"

"We'll give you fifty. But we both want a turn."

"Fuck off."

"Don't get so upset, sweetheart. You should be happy anyone's interested in you."

"Get lost," I said, climbing across the orange mesh barrier and up to the front door.

"But you can pay for your condoms yourself," the elbow shouted.

I waited in the corridor for the mysterious van to drive off. This was the third time I had seen it in the vicinity of our building.

The van wasn't the only thing bugging me. The druggies downstairs had given me cause for concern, too; their garbled shouts would travel through the building, occasionally reaching up to the attic. You had to keep an eye out when you walked down the hallways to make sure you didn't get jumped. But the junkies had disappeared a week ago, at the same time as the bikes we had used for our painting gigs. We had stored them in an empty apartment three stories above the drug addicts' hangout. Apparently it hadn't made any difference. Junkies were better than bloodhounds at sniffing out anything that could be converted to cash.

They hadn't dared set foot near the attic since the day one of their buddies' explorations led him too close to the Ice Cave. Verboten sent him tumbling down the stairs and threatened to switch out their junk for rat poison when they were too high to know the difference.

Up in the Ice Cave, Vorkuta had joined the group at Lion Killer. Smew and Alyosha were clipping and uploading different versions of the train video and adding links to it all over the Internet. They had concealed our location by making sure any potential trails led to the Sardinian mountain village of Orgosolo.

The digital footprints of our previous graffiti video passed through Easter Island.

Smew was wearing his favorite black Secundas T-shirt. It was cribbed from a uniform for Securitas, the global security company. Securitas had three bright-red balls above its name. The Secundas logo was in the same font, but the two balls at the sides had turned into Pac-Man figures that were gobbling the ball in the middle.

I left the guys their coffees; Alyosha was the only one who smiled and thanked me. Vorkuta and Smew didn't even look up from their screens.

"That white van was here again," I said.

"What did they want?" Vorkuta asked, without lifting his head.

"Pussy."

I collapsed on my mattress and listened to the tapping keyboards, which occasionally intensified into sustained machine-gun fire. Alyosha came over to the door of the laundry room and lifted a thumb.

The guy was so pale he looked like he hadn't seen a day of sunlight in his life; his face gleamed in the darkness like a white blob. He claimed that he'd been exposed to too much radiation as a child, like Obelix falling into the cauldron of magic potion in the Gaulish village. His skin didn't brown even if he was out in the sun all day. It didn't burn; it didn't tan. Alyosha was originally from Pripyat, the reactor city.

His dad had been a fireman; he died trying to put out the fire at Reactor 4 after it blew. Alyosha had been three years old at the time. He remembered sitting in the legendary Ferris wheel there; photographs of the amusement park had come to symbolize the destruction caused by the nuclear power plant. The city officials had opened the park after the accident so children would have something to do and families wouldn't panic. *The situation is under control,* they said, passing out cotton candy to the kids. Admission was free and the lines were long. Alyosha said he still remembered to this day waving to his mother from a dizzying height. For a three-year-old, ten meters is a dizzying height. He had seen the glow of the reactor on the horizon; his mother told him it was a fireworks show.

Vorkuta whistled over by the computers; Alyosha went back to confer with him and Smew in a low voice. They were a tight-knit family. During our weeks in Pripyat I had felt like an outsider more than once, despite the fact that Smew called me one leaf of our four-leaf clover one day when he noticed I was listening. I was an orphan their family had taken in out of pity.

I once asked Vorkuta why he walked with a limp. He thought for a moment and decided to answer, even though he didn't like talking about it. He had an Estonian mother and a Russian father, and he was originally from some tiny town that didn't even have a train station. One day, urged by a friend, he had grabbed his paint cans and headed to the big rail yards outside Saint Petersburg. He climbed up to the roof of a train before anyone could warn him. An old woman with a scarf around her head waved her hands furiously at him from the side of the track; Vorkuta just thought she was some crazy lady. "I should have listened to Grandma," he admitted. An arc of light shot up. A 25,000-volt current was running through the overhead wires; Vorkuta had flown three meters down to the tracks.

He was unconscious in the hospital for five days, and when he finally woke up, one hand was handcuffed to the iron bed and one leg was stretched up toward the ceiling. Plus he was facing demands for astronomical compensation—not for painting the freight train, but because the shock that almost killed him cut off electricity to half of Saint Petersburg. There was no guard in the room at night, the assumption being that a broken leg and handcuffs were enough to keep him confined.

But Alyosha was in the next bed over, undergoing cancer tests. The two of them immediately hit it off. Alyosha lifted a hacksaw blade from the toolbox of a maintenance man two floors down. Vorkuta sawed through one of the bars of his iron bed and fled the city on his still-broken leg.

That was the first time he had visited Pripyat, where he spent two months. Alyosha fished for the both of them from the Pripyat River. He had returned to the city of his birth to die. But he didn't; the tumor the doctors had been watching proved benign.

Vorkuta's leg didn't heal properly. That was why he limped when he walked; the limp wasn't as noticeable when he ran.

One hot day in Pripyat, I had been aghast when Vorkuta stripped off his shirt. The guy had three spines. One was the real deal, the second was a broad scar the train tracks had gouged into his skin, and the third had been seared into his flesh by the electric current.

I never asked Verboten what had happened to him, even though compared to Vorkuta his face looked like a mask from a horror movie. And Vorkuta had taken 25,000 volts.

Chain-link fences and abandoned buildings are tough on clothes, and I was sitting on my mattress, sewing up a ripped seam in my jeans. I thought it was a better alternative than Smew's strategy of patching his pants with a stapler.

Smew and I had been given a room to share; it was the building's former laundry, located in the attic. Massive, empty concrete basins still stood there, with a drain in the middle of the floor. At night the drain gurgled, even though there wasn't supposed to be any water in the building.

The narrow windows were high up on the wall, and all I could see was a strip of sky. At times the strip was blue, at others pearl gray. Once, a bolt of lightning flashed across my slice of heaven, and the washbasins echoed dully with the rumble of thunder.

A sharp tap from above startled me, and I jabbed the needle into my finger. A sparrow with a crooked beak was at the window, messaging me in Morse code: *Yo, lady. Give me seeds!*

In the afternoon Verboten returned to the attic. My fingers were full of holes, and the sole ray of sunlight had slid down the wall. He came and went without explaining himself. We paid our rent by helping him carry out the graffiti missions he planned.

Including us, there were about a dozen crews in Berlin. We painted whatever we wanted, wherever we wanted. The power to decide what the city looked like rested in our hands.

There was only a limited amount of respect to go around in the city's graffiti scene, and we wanted as hefty a chunk of it as possible. Or Verboten did, but it's not like I was complaining.

The biggest, most prominent crew was 1UP, One United Power. They put a lot of effort into spreading videos of their work online, and they traveled all over Europe, from Lisbon to Vienna. They even painted on other continents. Their MO was to head down into subway tunnels and paint parked trains underground.

They had a huge head start, so we had some catching up to do. But Verboten thought we had a better story. While 1UP bombed three boring letters in a thousand different places, we brought snow and ice and rats everywhere we went. Every time we painted, the result was unique. If you'd seen one 1UP video, you'd seen them all: a group of guys opens a manhole, drops into a metro tunnel, and paints an off-duty train in the dark. Sometimes they climb over a chain-link fence and someone's pants rip. Watching ten videos like that made you feel like Grandma dozing off in her rocking chair.

Verboten planned our graffiti strikes. If 1UP painted a train that was already parked, we'd pull an emergency brake while it was going full speed, jam the doors, and paint until we were forced to run. If 1UP painted in the dark, we'd paint during the day.

It wasn't just about painting a train and uploading the video. For us, the most important thing was how brazen we were. Anyone—well, not *anyone*—could paint a train at the station or rail yard the way I used to. Hidden from view.

We wanted to show we were the best. Not bold and beautiful, but ugly, dirty, and mean. We were waging a war over who ran the city and its public spaces.

Among graffiti artists, the highest part of a wall is called a heaven spot. The only way you can paint a heaven spot is to hang upside down over the edge of the roof while a friend holds you by the legs. Heaven spots have the best visibility from all across the city.

Verboten wanted to expand the concept of the heaven spot. For him, a heaven spot was any hella visible piece of graffiti. As Verboten saw it, this used to be a train that traveled around the city, advertising the crew that had painted it to tens of thousands of commuters. Nowadays it was a recording of a balls-out burn, a video clip that stood out from the crowd, spreading online to millions and millions of pairs of eyes.

Verboten promised that within a couple of months we'd rule not only Berlin's heaven spots, but those of Europe and the whole world.

We would be known as the elite team of graffiti artists.

The Ice Rats. We painted with icy colors and came from the north. Verboten was the only exception. I didn't know anything about his origins; he said he had moved so many times he wasn't from anywhere. But since he's the one who came up with the name Ice Rats, he was obviously happy to identify as one.

So I had become an Ice Rat. A rat. Back in Finland, the word *rat* had meant one thing and one thing only: the security guards who hunted us down. And here we were, voluntarily calling ourselves rats, even though we were writers. The world had turned upside down.

I shook my head. The sparrow had appeared again, drumming its beak against the window. It felt like it was trying to pound sense into me. *You're not going to think about Finland now, Metro.*

I was young and free, and no one could stop me. They could all go screw themselves. Except my friends.

I had almost forgotten Rust. I had decided to forget Rust.

Sometimes when I was dreaming I'd wake up to the sight of Rust falling in front of me, flailing and flailing and trying to fly like a baby bird but smacking into the asphalt, breaking every bone in his body while security guards watched from above. *Respect,* they'd say and laugh. I'd have to stare at the concrete wall of the laundry room for ages before the faces and uniforms of the guards would fade and the ice-skating rat that was really painted there gradually came into view.

MINUS 12 HOURS

"I have to go out for a minute. I need to get a new carrier pigeon. The old one's getting a little slow." I had found a pigeon skeleton in the back of the attic; I held it up in front of Verboten's face.

"Don't take too long. Remember, you have a job tonight," Verboten said, without glancing at me and my skeleton. He was concentrating on cutting a stencil out of paper.

"You've reminded me three hundred times."

"Three, max."

I left the Ice Cave, sliding the plywood covering the hole in the attic wall and slipping through the gap.

I balanced ten meters across a beam barely wider than my shoe. The beam was the sole reminder that a floor had once existed at this end of the attic. A chasm opened up below, with the remnants of demolished stories jutting out into it like fangs. If I fell, it would be close to a twenty-meter drop, and I'd be lucky if I somersaulted all the way to the bottom. It was far more likely that I'd be speared on the way down by rebar, jagged boards, or pipes sticking out of the devastated walls, floors, and ceilings.

Part of the roof had also collapsed, and in rainy weather the beam was as slippery as the rocks at the shore. Like that time when I was a kid and I slipped into the frozen sea before I knew how to swim.

I splashed around in the icy slush, frantically trying to find a foothold on the slick granite. Mom dashed down to help me and slipped in at the same spot. There we were, the two of us thrashing around in the frigid water. A guy who was walking his dog managed to fish us out.

The first week I lived in the attic, I would only straddle my way across, hugging it with both arms, advancing a few inches at a time. Vorkuta had snorted at my caution. He hopped across the beam on one foot, drunk off his ass.

"For keeping out trespassers it's better than the best heavy-duty padlock," was how Verboten boasted about his steel beam. "It's supposed to scare the crap out of anyone who sees it. The junkies would never be able to make it across."

I reached the iron door at the other end of the beam; luckily it opened into the stairwell. I flew down the stairs; I was late.

An old woman was sweeping the second-story landing. She had her hair tucked under a flowered scarf and was wearing a fur coat. The first few weeks I lived in the Ice Cave I thought she was a cleaning lady or something. But she had lived in the building for over forty years, the only one of the previous occupants who had stayed behind. Attempts had been made to move her out; Verboten said she had been offered apartments in several different neighborhoods. She had always refused, just snorted and slammed the door in the face of the briefcase-bearing company representative.

Verboten called her American Buffalo. She was stubborn as hell and wore a fur coat summer and winter.

As the furrows in American Buffalo's face deepened, the building around her crumbled. She tried to slow the decay by keeping the place sparkling clean. She had probably already scrubbed through the floors of her apartment; that's why she had moved on to scouring the corridor outside.

"Don't stay out too late," she called out in a feeble voice as I stepped past. This was her standard line. She said it every time I saw her, whether I was coming or going.

There was something creepy about American Buffalo; I had secretly spied on her from above. She'd systematically proceed along the second-floor hallway with her broom, sweeping back and forth. From time to time she'd pause to spray lavender scent into the air. She didn't set foot on the other floors; they were full of trash and dust and stank of piss. From time to time American Buffalo would stop, sigh, draw her fur coat more tightly around her, bite her lower lip, and continue on.

Out on the street, I hopped on a tram heading toward the river. A young woman was standing at a street corner in a threadbare bathrobe; she was talking to herself and tossing her head from side to side. Passersby gave her a wide berth. On the river, a tourist boat slid past between the warehouses. The passengers on deck snapped photos as the multilingual commentary echoed back from the display windows of a mobile phone store, like it was the Tower of Babel. I jumped off and darted between cars as I ran across a parking lot.

The train tracks curved out ahead to my right; a parade of cafes, pubs, kebab joints, and hole-in-the-wall Asian restaurants marched to my left. Each had a cluster of plastic tables and chairs out front, and over the months, the chairs had reproduced and gotten mixed up. They were like the rabbits we used to have when I was a kid.

Mom and Dad had dreamt of running an organic farm. Kind of like *Little House on the Prairie*, Mom's favorite series from her childhood, except that this house was at the edge of a forest, and it was drafty and full of holes and it slouched to one side. Mom had bought half a shed's worth of seeds she'd planned on planting into a lovely garden. Dad's job was to straighten out the crooked house. I was in charge of the rabbits. The idea was to keep the girl bunnies and boy bunnies in separate cages and let them out in turns to feed on the grass. First the girls, then the boys. But it took way too much time: the rabbits nibbled lazily at dandelions, and I was in a hurry. I would let them out at the same time and toss them back at random, equal numbers in each cage. Over the following months I got a better lesson in the effects of over-population than I ever would have had at school.

Walking along the sidewalk, scents flooded out of each doorway I passed: citrus, roasted coffee, crepes, cumin, grilled chicken.

It wasn't until my stomach growled that I realized how hungry I was. Since we'd burned the train I hadn't eaten anything except the small sandwich that morning.

A man with red cheeks had set up his sausage stand a little ways off, along the path leading to Friedrichshain Station. His plumpest wursts were as thick as his forearm, which had plenty of meat on it. One long sausage spiraled like a crown; he expertly cut chunks from it for his customers. One lady sporting a lavender suit jacket shoved a fat hunk into her tiny silver purse, straining the seams.

I hung out near the sausage stand to sniff away my hunger and keep one eye on the station platforms. A commuter train had just pulled in from Alexanderplatz, and people were streaming up the overpass stairs. The fastest had already made it across the overpass and were rushing past the sausage stand. A trembling man carried a single bicycle wheel, stroking its spokes, as if he were carrying a dead child.

Dad was one of the last to arrive. He looked more downtrodden than usual today. When he reached the sausage stand, he turned up his nose at the wax paper and rubbish strewn around. He didn't stop to pick it up today; a lot of times he did.

I didn't remember Dad being a pedantic neat freak. The belongings in our crooked wooden house hadn't been kept on shelves; they'd been spread across the floor. Occasionally he'd let the bunnies in to hop around, even though we'd soon be swimming in rabbit pellets. He was no carpenter, and Mom was no gardener. She didn't manage to scythe any of the tall grass that nearly engulfed the house, or sow a single seed. Dad thought chaos was the natural order of things, while Mom preferred things tidy. That's something else my parents argued about before their divorce. One year, the first snow started drifting in through a hole in the roof. I remember them looking at the pile of snow on the floor and then spending half the day bickering about whose job it was to shovel it up. In the meantime, I climbed up to the roof and nailed a piece of plywood over the hole.

Little House on the Prairie, my ass. If Mom and Dad had been pioneers they would have been the first to croak, and, for a little while at least, the Wild West would have been a more peaceful place.

I stayed close to the sausage stand so Dad wouldn't notice me.

My caution was unnecessary. He hadn't recognized me the week before, when, in a moment of determination, I had given him the chance to experience the joy of realizing his daughter was finally here. *Not off in Finland, where you abandoned me, you prick.* On my very first day of school. It was a long goddamn wait, since you were the one who was supposed to pick me up. Fourteen years, give or take. You left me standing there on the school steps, curling and uncurling my freezing toes, long after all the other parents had come by and carted off their kids.

So excuse me if I didn't exactly believe it when the postcards you sent me later assured me that you wanted to see me more than anything else in the world.

I had observed Dad's arrival by train several times—always the same train, always the same time—and waited for a tiny hint of what I remembered him by most of all. Back then, Dad loved to laugh: at first his head would fly back, and then a long, low chuckle would well up from somewhere inside him. Mom used to say that Dad's guffaws warmed our drafty house better than the radiator.

Dad didn't laugh or smile these days. He looked shorter than before, and his gait was different. When I was a kid, it seemed like Dad strode halfway to heaven with every step. You never heard his footfalls, either; his long lope carried him forward as softly as a leopard. Sometimes we'd play a game where I'd go to the far end of the house, crouch down, hold my hands over my eyes, and press my ear to the plank floor. It was my job to listen for Dad's approach, point in the direction the leopard was coming from, and say, "Gotcha!"

I lost every time. Dad would always touch me before I heard the slightest creak. He knew how to avoid the loose planks.

Nowadays Dad clomped; I could hear the sound of his combat boots pounding the asphalt from miles away.

Smile, I muttered at his back. *Smile, just once.*

He stopped at his regular cafe near the train station, ordered a coffee, and somberly sat down at the corner table, his usual spot for people watching.

I had ventured into the cafe the week before and taken a seat at the next table over. Dad had turned toward me three times. He looked right at me and then right through me, without any hint of recognition.

Today, I waited for Dad to drink his coffee in tiny gulps, like a sparrow sipping from a puddle. He rose from the table and left without saying good-bye to anyone.

I followed his ponderous footfalls to the next corner and stayed there, leaning against a lamppost. I knew where he was heading. He lived half a kilometer away, on the third floor of a verdigris apartment building. I'd snuck into the building opposite a few times, made myself comfortable on the ventilation balcony one floor down, and watched a window-size slice of his life. Dad seemed to spend most of his time sitting in front of the TV. There was no sign of other life in the apartment except the goldfish he'd occasionally feed in its bowl by the window.

Today I gripped the lamppost and watched Dad fade into the distance.

I could have taken the lack of laughter and the plodding. The main thing that kept me from establishing contact with Dad was his outfit.

From his belt hung pepper spray, a collapsible baton, and handcuffs, the way a headhunter displayed the scalps of his victims.

Dad had joined the profession I hated and feared most in this world. The profession that had killed Rust. The profession I wished I could forget but made me bite my cheeks until my mouth filled with blood any time I happened to run into a person dressed like Dad on the sidewalk.

Dad had become a graffiti artist's worst enemy.

He was a security guard.

MINUS 8 HOURS

I stopped on my way back to the Ice Cave. I sat down next to a storm drain, dropped pebbles in through the cracks, and listened to how long it took for them to plop into the water. When I was little, Dad used to tell me the story about an underground kingdom with castles and princesses and monsters; storm drains were the gateways to this magical land.

Dad told me lots of stories. He didn't tell much else.

The downstairs door of our half building was open. That should have put me on guard.

When I entered the dim hallway my foot knocked into a beer can and sent it spinning across the lobby. No one from the Ice Cave left their cans on the lower landing. The junkies were gone, and American Buffalo didn't leave garbage around.

I had only taken five steps before someone grabbed me from behind and started choking me. A second figure emerged from the shadows.

"Not much of a mansion you have here," he said.

I was struggling in vain; the grip was solid. The guy in front of me was wearing sunglasses, even though the hallway was dark.

"What's a girl doing on her own in such a big building?" he said. "Wouldn't it be polite for you to invite some guests over?"

I tried to answer, but the hand was choking me so hard that all I could do was wheeze.

"Abandoned buildings aren't safe places for girls on their own," he continued.

From his voice and green coat, I knew it was the guy who had catcalled at me from the white van earlier that day.

"We'll be happy to move in with you. At least for a couple of hours."

The guy choking me bit my earlobe and fumbled with the zipper on my jeans.

"Your mattress is pretty pounded out," said the guy with the sunglasses as he opened a door. "You have a lot of visitors here?"

His buddy dragged me into the junkies' pad.

"You piss in the corner? That's fucking disgusting. Haven't you ever heard of a bathroom? We figured you'd never heard of condoms, either, so we brought our own."

He didn't have the chance to say anything else before an iron pipe came crashing down on his back. Verboten had appeared in the doorway, his scarred face burning bright red.

I could feel the hand choking me ease off; Verboten was whaling away with the pipe. I heard a cry and a thud. I saw one figure scramble out the door, then the other, Verboten in pursuit. I heard another whack and a yelp from the lobby.

"Sorry, man, we didn't know she was your whore," the guy in the green coat shouted from the street. "How much do you want for her?"

It was quiet then. Verboten came into the junkies' pad and helped me up from the stained mattress.

"You all right?" he asked.

"I guess," I gasped. My throat hurt. I zipped up my pants. "It was the guys from the van."

"I don't know them," Verboten said.

I was chilling on my mattress in the Ice Cave. Verboten had sat down at my side for a moment; I had muttered a thank-you.

At the other end of the attic, Alyosha and Vorkuta were arguing over which year they had spent time in Orgosolo. The name made me think of the orcs from *The Lord of the Rings*.

I turned and looked at the wall of our laundry room, which was different from any other laundry room I had ever seen. In the few months I had spent in the Ice Cave, I had never grown tired of looking at it.

It was this wall that had inspired the name of our crew and of our home. The wall was covered by a piece four meters wide and two and a half meters tall. It was a wintry landscape including a rat skating across a frozen pond. The surface was covered by money that the rat was slicing with his skates. Pieces of banknotes drifted through the air with the snowflakes. The rat was holding a can of spray paint. Skating past a snowbank he had painted the words ICE RAT BANKSY.

Fucking Banksy, the most famous writer in the world. Everyone from the pope to Prince Charles knew Banksy these days. Or rather, they knew Banksy's works; Banksy kept his face hidden and his real name secret. Hollywood movie stars paid hundreds of thousands of dollars to hang a Banksy in their living rooms.

There was also a hole in the ice; a top hat floated on the water. Out of the blackness rose a banker's hand, a gold watch on the wrist.

Two things made the work unique. First, it was signed by Banksy. He hadn't signed many of his big pieces. According to Verboten, this one dated from the winter Banksy had spent painting in Berlin. It had snowed so much that year traffic had snarled as bus drivers abandoned their buses in favor of snowball fights. Folks had skied down Unter den Linden on Granddad's old wooden skis. The chancellor at the time, Gerhard Schröder, had been made into a snowman in front of the Bundestag, where it was promptly destroyed by the bomb squad because they were afraid its round belly concealed explosives.

The other unique thing about the painting in our laundry room was that it was in perfect condition. No one had sprayed anything over it. Banksy had hung out in the attic for a few weeks, dubbing it the Ice Cave because it was so drafty. The snow had gusted into the attic for days through the holes in the windows. One morning Verboten woke up to find his head frozen to the floor. They had to piss on it because there hadn't been any warm water upstairs. Verboten was proud that Banksy had been the one to piss his head free.

Inspired by the cold winter and the accommodations, Banksy had painted this self-portrait. He was the ice-skating rat giving money the finger.

Which is what we were doing, too: we were telling money to go screw itself.

But it wasn't something you could always afford to do.

Verboten appeared at the door to the laundry room. "Metro, it's time," he said. "Work calls."

Verboten had picked Alyosha and me to use the harnesses since we were the lightest ones in the crew. Alyosha looked like he had a chronic case of scurvy. Smew weighed about the same as me, it was true, but he was so clumsy that I didn't want him scrambling across roofs. He was as accident prone as he was chivalrous.

"Time to pay the rent," Verboten said.

He said the same thing every time we left to carry out some guerilla graffiti strike under his command.

"What rent?" I had asked the first time.

"Rent to make sure the demolition of the building doesn't continue," Verboten had snapped in a tone that blocked any further questions.

Smew explained to me later that Verboten had to pay bribes to make sure the apartment building stayed standing. And he had to do favors so people would do favors for us.

This was one of those times. We had to vandalize an ad on behalf of a competing car manufacturer. In return, our apartment building received a brief respite, and we had a free place to live. Now and again, big respectable firms paid graffiti crews to vandalize the work of other players in their industry. At its most rudimentary this meant scrawling dicks across billboards of smiling families buttering their bread at the breakfast table. But this job was going to be a little more complicated.

"Are you up for this?" Verboten asked, eyeing my trembling hands.

"Why wouldn't I be?" I snapped.

We rode a tram to the banks of the Spree and headed down the escalators leading to the metro. The tunnel smelled like someone had been burning tires in there. We changed lines and got off one stop before Potsdamer Platz; Verboten walked in front of Alyosha and me. At the corner he pointed at an office building rising before us. One facade was covered by a twenty-meter-tall ad for a hatchback; behind the car, images of mountains, desert dunes, a beach, a city skyline, and jungle vines had been Photoshopped into a massive collage.

"I've never done anything like this before," I said.

"None of us have," Verboten said. "Not many people in Berlin have. This is what they do in Brazil."

"I thought they played soccer in Brazil."

"The ones who don't make the soccer team do this. Pixadors. They don't even use safety harnesses. Piece of cake. They also stand on the roofs of trains traveling at full speed. That's a lot harder."

I eyed the vertical surface that stood before me like a cliff. I'd suffered from vertigo ever since what happened last fall. One foggy night in Finland, a guard had pushed me off the roof of this big building where they stored stage scenery. I'd been lucky to survive; I'd only dropped three meters to an overhang instead of falling the full twenty meters to the ground. But the Metro of a year ago—the girl who sprinted along the edges of roofs as nimbly as a chimney sweep, searching for heaven spots, without getting the least bit dizzy—was nothing but a memory.

Alyosha chewed his lip; his albino skin concealed how pale he had turned. Evening had fallen, but the wall and its ad glowed in the glare of spotlights as brightly as they did in daylight.

"Are you filming this?" I asked Verboten. "Will it make a better video if we come tumbling down?"

Verboten didn't answer. He turned the burnt side of his face toward me, so the drooping eyelid hid his eye. This meant he was done talking. He nudged my shoulder with his fist; that was the only good-bye we were going to get.

Alyosha and I were wearing white coveralls. We were carrying a couple of cans of paint and a canvas bag with paint rollers sticking out the top. In the lobby, we said the bathroom walls on the thirteenth floor had been vandalized, and we were there to remove any and all traces of damage.

"Zero tolerance," Alyosha said to the guard, who was sitting at his desk, measuring the distance between his forefinger and a fly dozing on the ceiling. "Any and all graffiti needs to be covered up immediately. Company policy. Good policy, too. Filthy goddamn swine."

The guard waved us toward the elevators. We checked ourselves in the mirror. Our coveralls were splattered with paint in every color of the rainbow. The name of our fictional employer, the Perfect Paint Company, was printed across the back, along with the logo: a brush and a roller set like crossbones. The same logo adorned our bag, which was jam-packed with spray paint underneath a paint-smeared roller tray, in two small backpacks.

Most of the time it was easiest to do everything out in the open and as obviously as possible. That aroused the least suspicion. The name of the company always changed, but we always stuck with the same game plan. If necessary, we were even prepared to hand out a business card with a company telephone number on it. The security guard or receptionist could call the main office if they wanted to. Verboten would answer at the other end, flipping through an imaginary list of customer orders and say that his painters were at the exact location indicated on the work order. Was there a problem? Had his staff behaved unprofessionally? The Perfect Paint Company paid particular attention to the social skills of its employees.

Verboten could talk a dead man back to life when he felt like it. He was the most presentable member of our crew, as long as you didn't see his face.

I pressed the button for the top floor. With his eyes big like Bambi's, Alyosha stared as the numbers above the door slowly changed; after the twelfth floor it jumped right to fourteen. We left the cans of paint and rollers and other extraneous supplies in a cleaning closet. We found the fire escape stairs, which took us one floor higher, and stepped out onto a narrow balcony.

The wind was blowing my hair in my face. The crowns of Tiergarten's trees loomed before us. Farther off, a hot-air balloon advertising beer glowed against the sky. It looked like we were even higher up.

"We never had to pay rent in Pripyat," Alyosha said.

"You really want to go back to that radioactive dump?"

"That dump is my hometown."

I peered over the edge at the rushing river of cars below. Headlights and streetlamps pierced the darkness.

"So this is where we're supposed to climb down?" I asked.

"Other side of the building," Alyosha said.

A narrow ladder rose from one end of the balcony. The ladder's rungs were covered by moss; no one seemed to have used it since the building was finished. Despite the beads of sweat rolling down my back, I was shivering.

"Ladies first," I said as Alyosha reached across the railing, shoving him out of the way. If I ended up behind Alyosha, I'd never have the guts to climb. Now at least I could pretend he'd catch me if I fell.

The ladder leaned away from the building. It felt like my back was parallel to the ground and I was being pulled down by the gravity of Jupiter. It's more than twice the gravity of Earth. That made me a 150-kilo fairy. The bag slid down from my shoulder and came to a stop hanging below me. My fingers slipped on the mossy sides of the ladder. I held on to them like a lifesaver; if I released my grip to climb up to the next rung I was sure I'd plummet to the ground.

"Come on, Metro, don't choke," Alyosha said.

I bit my tongue. The taste of rusty metal made my fingers work. I reached for the next rung up. I made it past the ledge and threw myself onto the roof.

We circled around to the far side of the building, checking for surveillance cameras the whole time. There weren't any. A flaccid dragon balloon bobbed at one corner of the roof; the string had caught on a bolt, and most of the helium had escaped. It was like the starving second cousin of the beer-hawking hot-air balloon. The wrinkly dragon halfheartedly tried to flap off; its scales were spotted gray from countless rains.

"Looks like an old graffiti artist," Alyosha said.

We stopped at the edge of the roof and gazed down at the ad below. The car was the size of a dinosaur; the ground was as far away as the moon.

"Fuck this. I'm not doing it," I said.

"When I was a kid I saw this one pirate movie where a guy fell from the mast," Alyosha said. "He plunged his knife into the mainsail and slid all the way down as smoothly as if he were taking an elevator. The blade split the sail."

"Is that the tactic you're planning on using here?"

"It wouldn't work, even with a sail. It was the same sort of Hollywood crap as someone flying backward when a bullet hits them. That doesn't happen. You drop dead in your tracks like a rag doll. There was this series we used to watch on Soviet TV that showed the different ways America tried to fool the rest of the world."

We tested the solidity of the ventilation ducts rising from the roof. They were nothing but sheet metal; they wouldn't even support Alyosha and his bird-bone frame. There was also a flagpole with no line. Based on how rusty it was, no one had ever used it. Alyosha wrapped his rope around it.

For my anchor, I chose an antenna leaning over on its side. I tested how sturdy it was by kicking the bottom. Blue sparks flew from it.

"You have a good chance of getting fried on the way down," Alyosha said, glancing over at me while I was dicking around.

"Hey, the most important thing here is the fucking rent. Who cares about third-degree burns?"

We took our backpacks out of the bag. I rolled up the bag and shoved it into my backpack, unzipped my coveralls, and tied the sleeves around my waist. We already had our harnesses on underneath our coveralls. I fumbled with the rope and knotted it through the carabiner. I strapped my backpack to my front so I could access more paint as necessary.

"Don't drop anything. You could kill someone walking below," Alyosha said.

The hardest part was taking that first step into the void. I had never rappelled before. Verboten had given us a quick course in the Ice Cave, answering our questions with *You learn by trying*.

I leaned back. Jupiter's gravity wasn't cutting it; I felt the sun exerting an inexorable pull on me. My weight multiplied thirty times as I extended myself over the edge.

Alyosha was already sliding down the wall five meters below me.

"Come on, we don't have time," he said. "Chop-chop."

I scooched myself lower, sure that the carabiner would give. I switched the can from hand to hand, making one huge letter after the other.

A flock of pigeons swirled up from the roof of the next building over; they arced past like a squadron of fighters on the attack. Gusts of air wafted against my face; the pigeons glared with red, unblinking eyes as their machine-gun wings said *Ratatatatatatat. Fall, Metro, fall.*

The rope slid more than I meant it to, and I slipped a couple of meters in one violent lurch.

"Faster," Alyosha shouted from lower down. "Girls always take so long."

The nozzle of my spray paint jammed. The faint shriek of a siren carried up from below. At the same instant, I hit a knot that had formed in the rope. My slide came to an abrupt stop. The can slipped from my hand and spun through the air.

There was no sound, but a red spot suddenly exploded on the asphalt, as if someone committing suicide had splatted there.

"Goddammit, I told you not to drop it," Alyosha hissed.

The pigeons flapped past the rising moon.

I leaned against a windowsill, managed to unravel the knot, and continued my descent. I probably should have checked the rope before

I started out. My fingers were dripping with sweat. The wailing siren got closer; I spotted a police car three blocks away, headed in our direction. The headlights of the vehicles below glowed and glared more penetratingly than the pigeons had just a moment ago.

In one window, some guy in a suit was squatting on his desk, filming me. I had drawn my shemagh over my head so only a sliver of my eyes was uncovered.

Three letters to go.

Alyosha was done with his bit. He twirled down headfirst in his harness like a bat. He liked wall climbing. His frail, wan appearance was deceptive; he had the biggest balls of any of us. He wasn't afraid of heights, enclosed spaces, dogs, radiation, snakes, water, anything. He had jammed his cans of spray paint into his backpack and was looking in the direction of the sirens. I finished writing my last letter and slid down next to him.

Now there were two police cars. They were stuck behind a truck that was backing up and blocking the street. One of the officers had climbed out of his car and was furiously waving at the truck to move.

"This rope is too short," Alyosha said.

I glanced down past my rear. I only had half a meter of rope left. Verboten had given us the hanks of rope and promised that they would be plenty long. *Just anchor the rope at the middle and come down.*

"We have to jump," Alyosha said.

"That's at least a four-meter drop," I squawked.

The truck had backed into a portico. The first police car steered around it. They were less than a block away.

Alyosha clicked himself out of his carabiner, dangled from the two rope ends to cut the distance, and dropped. He smacked down on top of the can I had dropped, or rather the paint splotch the can had left behind. His white coveralls were stained red, and when he stood up he looked like he was staggering down the sidewalk covered in blood. A woman pushing a stroller started screaming.

So much for discretion.

The doors to the first police car were open, and the police officers were weaving their way through the traffic with the two of us in their sights.

I freed myself from my rope, plunged through the air, and landed. My left ankle twisted under the pressure; it felt like someone had spiked a red-hot nail through it.

I limped and howled every time I put weight on the ankle. Alyosha wrapped his arms around me and staggered; I weighed more than he did. A guy drenched in blood was dragging a screaming woman around the corner. People gladly made way for us. We went down into the metro tunnel, passed through it, and emerged on the other side of the street.

The first police officer had disappeared; three others swarmed the front of the building, milling around under the still-swinging ropes.

Four vertical columns of letters ran down the giant billboard. I had sprayed two of them. From left to right they read:

THE CAR OF CHOICE FOR
BABY KILLERS
GUN RUNNERS
GENOCIDAL MANIACS

Verboten had told us that the car company's factories also made parts that were sold to the Syrian government, ISIS terrorists, and a couple of African despots who killed their subjects with zero remorse. Our message was a voice crying out in the wilderness against the heartlessness of the business world.

My heel banged against a stair. I screamed in agony. Alyosha pulled me into a small grocery store. He circled behind the meat counter, apologizing profusely, and dragged me through the back room; a clerk with a walrus moustache cursed and chased us and kept saying we weren't allowed back there.

"You're the one who's always digging through the trash," he shouted. He thought we were druggies and didn't dare touch us, but he howled in our faces like the sirens outside.

Alyosha forced me to jump from the loading dock. The nail wasn't just being spiked through my ankle now; it was being driven up my entire leg. We hobbled across the yard and over the fence into another courtyard. In the corner there was a sandbox, in the sandbox a red plastic bucket. We passed through a junk-filled alleyway and out to the street. Alyosha helped me onto the first bus to come by; two police cars drove in the opposite direction, sirens blaring.

My ankle was swelling before my eyes.

MINUS 5 HOURS

The receptionist stuck her nose in the air, said I needed to show her a passport. The next thing I needed was an EU health insurance card or shitloads of money. Alyosha raised his voice and asked about the doctor's professional ethics, which was when two security guards appeared from the bowels of the building.

We left. I leaned on Alyosha as we made our way down the dark streets. He called Verboten from his cell phone. Verboten told us where to find a place that offered care to immigrants. I had to wait my turn. Alyosha headed out to hunt down something to drink; our throats were bone dry from the job.

The doctor's illuminated door had a ten-meter nimbus. Behind its green surface, treatment was being administered to someone I couldn't see but could hear all the same. The voice howled until it broke, as if the patient were being skinned alive.

A child was led past me by the hand. His head was wrapped in a heavy towel; blood was slowly seeping through the linen. He stared straight ahead, his face milky white, red rings around his eyes. The mother softly hummed a lullaby that mentioned *ölüm* several times. I knew enough Turkish to understand that the song was about death. I recognized the word for death in thirty languages.

The nurse knocked on the doctor's door; it opened a crack. The agonized cries carried into the corridor with even more dreadful force. But the boy and his mother were denied entry. After being turned away, they sat down across from me.

The mother was taking off the boy's shirt so it wouldn't get any bloodier. Her fingers trembled as they unbuttoned it.

Everything around me seemed to be a reflection of the pain in my leg. Someone was screaming behind a door. The pale child was staring at me, mute and solemn. The blood oozing out from the towel turban trickled down his bony shoulders to his chest, which was as pale as his face. The red rivulets of blood flowed into each other like the roots of pine trees; blue veins gleamed through the skin of his stomach. The mother tenaciously hummed her lullaby, eyes glistening.

Alyosha returned with a cup of coffee. He had to walk several blocks to find us something to drink. The coffee had cooled on the way.

Inside the doctor's office, the screams had faded to moans.

We sat there face-to-face without talking, like a couple. A shiver ran up my spine every time a startling screech lashed out from the office. The mother had tired of humming; a tic danced in her left eye in time to the screeches.

By the time I finally made it to see the doctor I'd decided I wouldn't scream no matter what happened or how bad it hurt. The doctor was a small, timid-looking man who seemed to have been more traumatized by the agonized screams of the previous patient than those of us in the waiting room had been. He touched my ankle as cautiously as you'd touch crystal; he was afraid I might start shrieking, too. He suspected that I had stretched, or possibly torn, a ligament but couldn't completely rule out the possibility of a fracture. The X-ray equipment would be available in four hours—could I come back then? They needed to take an image of my ankle before they made any final decisions. He told me to go home in the meantime and sent me packing with two tablets to ease the pain.

Alyosha promised to walk me to the Ice Cave and back. But trudging through the streets felt like too much; I parked myself on a bench in the waiting room and lay down.

"Come on," Alyosha urged.

"I can't."

"I hate hospitals."

"This isn't a hospital. This is a hallway. There are a million goddamn hallways in this world."

We looked on in silence as the next man was taken in to see the doctor; a bone in his forearm was sticking through the fabric of his shirt. He jabbered that he had just been trying to change the television channel.

"I'm serious, come on," Alyosha whispered.

I rolled my coveralls up into a pillow under my head and turned toward the wall. That's what Dad used to do whenever he'd settle down for his nap. At first he took his siestas in the bedroom. Then Mom told him that healthy men don't spend their days lounging around; the house would fall down around our ears if he spent all day in bed. Dad answered that it may very well fall down around our ears since it'd been crooked from the moment we set foot in it. They started arguing. I remembered the shouting; I was only six years old at the time. Their shrieking had been more excruciating to my ears than what I'd been hearing coming from the doctor's office. Dad had picked up a stained sofa at the flea market and started dozing on that during the day instead of the bed. Mom would stomp back and forth in protest, clatter our only pot against its lid and go on and on about how a house of sloth was doomed to destruction. Then she would vacuum under the sofa, banging it against the couch's feet. Dad would turn his back to whatever was going on in the living room and lower a palm over his ear.

This is how I remember Dad: hand covering his ear, back to me, the shirt that was a little too short revealing the bumps of the vertebrae of his lower back. I would touch them gingerly; for me, they were mountains.

The last thing I had seen and felt of my father had been his vertebrae. Then he vanished, and it was fourteen years before I saw him again. In Berlin, wearing the uniform of a security guard.

Now I was treating Alyosha the way Dad had treated Mom. I turned my back to his whining; I refused to leave with him. I shielded my ear with my hand so I wouldn't have to listen.

Alyosha tugged at my shirt. Then he pushed me. I didn't budge. Alyosha didn't weigh much. That was the last time I saw him alive. And I didn't even see him; I felt him. I felt the hammering of Alyosha's bony hands.

MINUS 1 HOUR

My ankle was x-rayed the next morning. I had a hard time understanding the doctor's broken English. No bones were broken. Apparently the ligament was partially torn, and I might be looking at an operation, or I might not. The nervous little doctor had been exchanged for a taller one; he had a spongy handshake and eyes that looked past me, toward the shadow flickering against the wall to my left. He spoke in the third person, as if he were addressing my shadow, not me.

"She needs to stay off her feet for next days. She needs to rest a leg and not put any weight on it. It's important that she allows time for the swelling to go down and she doesn't make injury worse. Does she understand?"

My shadow didn't respond.

I got crutches that, based on their condition, some German soldier from the forests of Teutoburg must have used to bludgeon the life out of Roman legionnaires in the year 9 AD. Both were scuffed and dented, and I couldn't adjust them. There was a permanent height difference of ten centimeters between them.

The person in charge of the supply room was a woman with a bob. Her face screwed up in a fake smile when she opened her mouth. She refused to exchange the crutches, or even just one of them, so I could get two of the same height.

"They worked perfectly well when I handed them to you. Did you break them already? If so, you're responsible for replacing them."

Her smile could have crushed granite into gravel.

I started lurching down the street. I didn't have any cash, but I took a seat on the commuter train anyway. A couple of stations later, a ticket inspector climbed aboard. I'm usually fast enough to slip out the closest exit. This time I wasn't. The inspector asked for my personal information and demanded I pay the fare.

I said my permanent address was in Pripyat, Ukraine, and offered the street and the number of the apartment building where I'd stayed, in the heart of the deserted city. I did not offer that the only other occupants of said city, aside from my friends, had been rats and bats and the occasional fox. The inspector made me get off at a stop that was two kilometers away from the Ice Cave.

I slowly hobbled up the hill. The two kilometers felt like twenty. The doctor had ordered me to keep my leg horizontal as much as possible, and now I understood why. With every step, the blood packed in the twisted ankle, and the throbbing intensified exponentially.

When I finally made it to my street I took a break before I started climbing the stairs. I leaned against the low iron railing. Someone had locked a bike to the streetlamp with three locks and then swathed the whole thing in plastic wrap. It looked like the silk-wrapped prey of a giant spider, but, hey, there was no way anyone could steal it quickly. That's how we should have locked up our bikes so the junkies wouldn't have snagged them.

A light-blue VW Beetle raced past like a piece of sky on the lam.

I watched the shoes of the other pedestrians walking by. My footwear of choice was rubber-soled tennis shoes that didn't slip on metal roofs and walls. Now I envied the women clacking along in their high heels, ankles rolling lightly back and forth without their owners collapsing and holding their legs, wailing.

I would have preferred to spend all day sitting there on the railing. But I was going to have to climb the stairs sometime. I decided to wait until a truck that was blocking the entrance moved out of the way.

I shut my eyes, and, even though it was only a couple of minutes, I almost dozed off. The truck's engine started up; I opened my eyes wide enough to watch the truck advance almost as slowly as me on my bum leg. It avoided the bumps and potholes in the road as if it were transporting a load of crystal chandeliers. I waited until I saw it turn the corner. I decided to take it easy until the final blast of exhaust had dissipated.

Eventually I was out of excuses. I started climbing.

Every footfall was agony. I dug into the pocket that held the pain pills the doctor had given me. I hadn't taken them in the middle of the night, and I wasn't about to take them now, either. As long as I was in pain, I knew I was alive.

When I got to the second-floor landing American Buffalo was there, sweeping away.

She gave me the usual greeting: "Don't stay out too late."

"It's only nine in the morning, goddammit," I snapped at the old hag. I normally didn't say anything to her.

"Too late," she repeated, giving me a long stare. "You're too late."

Then American Buffalo grabbed my hand and squeezed; I squealed and wrenched free. Red gouges had appeared in my wrist; blood was oozing out of one.

"Crazy old bat," I barked. "I'm not your daughter."

"You're late," she muttered in response.

I hopped to the top of the stairs, slipped between the boards and under the VERBOTEN tape, and crossed the hole-riddled treads to the fire door leading to the attic. I fished out the key from under the stairs; it dangled above the chasm of collapsed floors on a three-meter fishing line.

I opened the fire door. I realized that crossing the beam to the Ice Cave with crutches in both hands would be a challenge.

I shoved the crutches into my armpit, leaned out over the beam, my legs straddling it, and scooched across to the other side. The trip took longer than it used to, and teetering across with my legs spread made me dizzier than walking upright.

The sweat was making my eyes sting. When I tried to wipe my forehead, one of the crutches slipped. I only just caught it and almost lurched halfway off the beam as I did.

Heart pounding and hands slipping, I kept heading for the brick wall.

Our door of brick-camouflage plywood was missing.

I shoved the crutches through the gap in the wall and then crawled in. I immediately banged my injured ankle against the edge of the hole, and then I bashed it again as I stood up.

"Who invented corners?" I shouted. "Who's the idiot who thought putting corners in this fucking building was a good idea?"

No one answered. All I could hear was the blood rushing in my ears.

I took a few steps before the crutch slipped from my grasp and my good foot slid out from under me. As I fell, black lightning flashed across my eyes.

I lay there cursing and blaming everything around me: the traffic signs that, for some incomprehensible reason, Verboten had collected to cover the attic walls; Rust for dying and leaving me to live in a ramshackle place like this; the crumbling bricks, the holes in the floors, and Smew for thinking this was a romantic place to stay because he loved old, dilapidated, abandoned buildings more than he loved actual breathing humans. I cursed every person who had set foot in this attic over the past hundred years and every pigeon that had ever crapped on the building's eaves and every chimney sweep who had ever climbed up to the roof to swab out the building's flues.

No one answered. It was almost pitch black; the only light came from the gap in the wall I had entered through. The shaft of light hit the traffic sign for GENERAL DANGER, which stared back at me, an expressionless black vertical line. The UNEVEN ROAD sign showed off its mounded décolletage. Verboten said it meant beware of milk-maids up ahead.

I was lying in something wet.

I fumbled my way over to the light switch and flicked it in vain. It was only now I realized that a familiar, soothing hum was missing; the computers weren't on.

I squinted. I had slipped in a puddle. I could make out the dark footprints of my tennis shoes near it.

I licked my wet fingertips; they tasted like the rusty rocker panel of an old hot rod.

My headlamp was in the laundry room. I hobbled in through the darkness; the pain surged between my ankle and my head like swells on an open sea. There was no land in sight; I rose and fell from one wave to the next, bobbing on my ankle.

I found the laundry room door. I groped around my mattress for the headlamp. All I could feel were lumps, the same ones I felt when I was lying on it. I hopped over to Smew's mattress on one leg. The lamp was under his pillow of folded newspaper. I clicked it on and the light gleamed weakly. Smew had used it again, the dickhead. He had been borrowing it ever since we'd left Finland, even though he didn't read. He just wanted a night-light on whenever he was alone.

The only thing he used to be afraid of was water. Then this one security guard back in Finland tried to kill him in a dark, abandoned building. So these days he was afraid of the dark, too.

Two timid bunnies slept shivering side by side in the laundry room, taking turns having nightmares.

I was the one who was always stealing new batteries for the lamp. There was a heap of used ones next to Smew's mattress.

I turned the headlamp on high. Chunks of concrete littered the floor; something was drifting through the air, making me cough harder and harder. Flakes of what looked like gold were floating in the beam of light.

I hobbled forward.

Smew wasn't under his balled-up blanket.

"Smew," I said.

My voice didn't echo back the way it normally did in the laundry room.

I headed for the opposite wall and thrust my hand through the cloud of dust in front of my face. It didn't hit anything. Banksy's work had disappeared.

The entire wall had vanished.

GROUND ZERO

I groped through the gap in the wall and into the main room of the attic. The gleam of the headlamp reflected back from the nearest traffic signs; they glimmered like round-headed ghosts. They watched me make my way to the deepest corner of the Ice Cave, where a few travel trunks contained the moth-eaten rags of long-ago evacuated residents' ancestors.

The biggest, darkest trunk was always empty, except for the blanket at the bottom. This was where Verboten slept. He was a fan of Dracula movies where vampires dozed the day away in coffins. Verboten thought graffiti artists and vampires had a lot in common when it came to sleep patterns.

Next to the trunk, Verboten had set out a five-branched brass candelabra he had found in a wooden crate: he lit it whenever he retreated to his bed. He had covered the low attic windows with dark cardboard.

Our entire attic, our Ice Cave, had been darkened using the same technique. Outsiders could not be allowed to see that the partially demolished building was still inhabited.

I knocked on Verboten's coffin and lifted the lid. He wasn't home.

I aimed the headlamp at the corners; the light flickered. My foot ached.

I climbed into the trunk, curled up, and fell asleep.

When I woke up, it was still dark. It was always dark in the Ice Cave. The computers still weren't on. I called out. No one answered. This wasn't unusual. Smew and Alyosha often worked with their headphones on.

My legs were stiff from lying in the trunk; I tottered over to the light switch on my crutches. The electricity still wasn't working. My headlamp was getting weaker; it kept fading in and out like a fatigued firefly.

There was a strange smell in the Ice Cave.

I made my way over to the wall and tore at a piece of cardboard covering one of the narrow windows. Verboten had firmly secured it to the wall with layers of duct tape. He would have been in his element putting up blackout curtains during a war. I had no doubt he could make entire cities disappear from the view of nighttime onlookers.

I managed to rip the cardboard away from one of the upper corners, using one of my crutches to twist it down the rest of the way. Daylight flooded the attic. The sun was so high, it was as if I had stepped out of a pitch-black basement directly into bright sunlight. I had to squint. Daylight is a graffiti artist's worst enemy. We're cave trolls who emerge when night falls and scurry back to our holes before dawn to escape the sun's scorching rays.

I turned around and gasped.

The metal desktop towers had been wrenched apart and the hard drives removed, the remainder of their guts smashed to bits.

The puddle I had slipped in was clearly visible now. It gleamed on the floor in a round, red pool; a long gash across it showed the spot where I had slipped. The pool was like a traffic sign that had been hammered into the floor. Dark crimson, through and through.

In the corner, near the entrance, stood another puddle, bigger. The surface of this one seemed to be alive. I made my way closer. It was seething with bees, drinking blood like there was no tomorrow.

The bees were partying.

The floor was full of bloody footprints and smudges. Some were from my shoes and crutches.

I crawled out through the entrance and onto the beam that spanned the void. I lay there on my stomach, looking down. Five floors below, among the rubble from the demolition, I saw two bodies sprawled. One was Alyosha. The face of the other one was crushed, but it was wearing a Secundas T-shirt.

Smew's arm had an extra joint in it. So did his leg.

My arms and legs were wrapped around the beam; otherwise I would have fallen.

I lay there, eyes closed, like a baby monkey clinging to a branch. I couldn't move forward, I couldn't move backward. Knocking me down from my rusty branch would have been a cinch.

I started when I heard a bang. I caught motion down below. Smew's hand was moving. He was alive.

I shouted down.

I realized too late that Smew's body was moving because someone was dragging it by the legs. A bald guy pounced out from the shadows and into the middle of the small, rubble-strewn courtyard, scanning up in the direction of my cry.

I pressed into the beam, trying to be the same size, not an inch wider.

The guy yelled over to the side without taking his eyes off the building. His buddy rushed past, presumably for the stairs.

I backed up along the beam and retreated into the Ice Cave.

The last thing I saw in the courtyard was the bald guy staring up and talking into his phone.

I headed for the window where I had torn off the blackout cardboard. On the way, I flipped over Lion Killer. The monitors crashed down; one tumbled across the floor like a ball rolling along a soccer field.

I reached down to one of the table's legs and grabbed a brick; the footsteps dashing up the stairs throbbed in my ears. I hobbled over to the uncovered window and smashed it with the brick. I knocked out the jagged shards so I wouldn't cut myself as I crawled through. I peered out. A pigeon's outraged, fire-red eye was glaring down at me. It was guarding a nest a meter up and would have been more than happy to peck out my eyes. Just like everything else in the vicinity, bird or mammal.

It was a meter and a half to the nearest ledge; if I could get a grip on it with my fingers, I could try to climb a bit of lightning rod attached to the wall and make for the roof.

A meter and a half. No sweat.

Except I would never make it with this ankle.

I picked up a shard of glass from the floor and sank the tip into my palm. When the blood oozed out, I reached out the window as far as I dared and pressed a bloody handprint into the wall halfway between the ledge and the window.

I stumbled back into the attic, limped over to the trunk Verboten used as his bed. I lay down on my back and lowered the crutches at my sides, like one of my Iron Age ancestors giving funeral gifts to a dead comrade, useful implements for their journey to the hereafter.

I closed the lid and lay there in the darkness I had created.

I decided death didn't scare me. I was already lying in a coffin, and I was already dead. It's a lot easier to be dead than alive. All you have to do is lie there. I let the blood flow out of my palm.

It wasn't long before I heard someone run across the floor.

THE COFFIN

At least two sets of frantic footsteps made for the middle of the attic.

Then it was quiet.

My foot was throbbing. My palm was throbbing.

Make some noise, goddammit.

I wondered how long the oxygen in the coffin would last.

My tailbone started to ache. I had shattered it after falling off a roof the previous fall, when I had been running from security guards, the ones who had killed Rust.

I had been knocked down.

Rust had been knocked down.

I heard rustling nearby. At least one of my pursuers was still in the attic. His footsteps approached the corner where the trunk sat.

I thought about my twisted ankle, my jacked tailbone, my bleeding palm, Rust. Back in Finland after a graffiti gig Rust and I would sometimes make a campfire in the old bunker. The woods were full of white flowers so tiny it took ten to cover Rust's thumbnail. I picked a bouquet of over a hundred twinflowers for him; it fit in the palm of my hand. We slept in the bunker. In the middle of the night when it grew cool I pressed up against Rust. He had fallen asleep with the bouquet clenched in his fist.

I could smell Rust in the trunk with me; his scent was a blend of paint, campfire, and twinflowers. The memory made my eyes sting. The footsteps stopped outside the trunk. I almost bit a hole in my lip as I held back tears.

This was it. So much for this amazing, shitty life.

A voice called out from the other side of the attic. The person standing next to me grunted and slowly made his way toward his partner. After a few seconds the footfalls disappeared. I didn't know if they'd actually left the attic, or if they were just waiting for me to emerge from my hiding place. The only thing I could hear was the throbbing in my palm.

A cry and a crash and curses rang out from the direction of the window.

The air was heavy. I tried counting to a hundred but I kept losing track.

I heard creaking and banging. The sounds were coming from inside the coffin. My numb legs were turning on their own without me realizing it; they had banged against the crutches.

I wouldn't be able to outrun a turtle right now.

What difference did any of this make? Wherever I went, I killed everything around me. It would be better if I died.

I angrily threw back the lid of the trunk so it rocked on its hinges. I tumbled out to the floor, grabbed my crutches, and lurched forward. It seemed like I was making as much racket as a small printing press.

The attic was empty. They had left, at least for the time being.

I looked into the laundry room. The wall on which Banksy had painted *Ice Rat* truly had vanished. It hadn't been smashed to bits. They had taken the Banksy with them.

I remembered the truck I had seen outside the building. The one that had driven very carefully, as if it had been transporting the queen's crystal. For as long and hard as I stared at it, I hadn't looked at the license plate number, not even once. I didn't even remember the color of the truck now.

I peered out the window I had smashed. My bloody, darkening palmprint emblazoned the wall like a Stone Age cave painting. The downspout outside the window hung loosely; someone had tried to climb out and follow me. They thought I'd made it to the roof and escaped that way.

I limped over toward the entrance of the Ice Cave, to the corner where a second broad pool of blood was spreading. It was covered with bees, but I still could make out a blurry reflection of my face on its dark red surface.

I had to find a way out of this valley of death. I crawled across the beam and opened the iron door. I hobbled past the gaping holes in the stairs and the chasm of the elevator shaft. I didn't dare look down. It was a well and my dead friends lurked at the bottom. If I looked in, one of them would grab me and drag me down to drown in the depths of death.

I limped over to the stairs.

Three floors down, American Buffalo was scouring the hallway.

"You're late," she said.

She pinched my cheek and shook it. That was all it took to send me to my knees. For a tiny woman, American Buffalo was surprisingly strong; her grip kept me from falling face-first to the floor. The last thing I remembered were her knobby fingers digging into my arms like the claws of a raven.

II: THE GIRL AND THE RAT

THE BRAID

I cracked my eyes. Delicate white sunbursts floated before me, surrounded by shimmering rays. I slowly raised my head. I was lying on a
bedspread. A quilt stitched together from dozens of swatches of fabric
in random colors had been pulled over my feet. I rose up on one elbow.
My right hand was bandaged; it looked like I was wearing a white
mitten.

What the hell had I been thinking, fucking up my right hand? The
one I paint with? That's kind of like a preacher cutting off his tongue.

Stupid Metro. You fucking idiot.

I was lying in a room twice as high as it was wide. The rose-pat-
terned wallpaper had a faded spot in the shape of a cross; a crucifix had
once hung there.

A cuckoo clock chirped eleven times in a nearby room.

A buffalo shambled past the doorway.

At a second glance, it turned out to be a woman bundled in fur.
American Buffalo.

She noticed I had woken and clucked her tongue sharply at my
attempts to climb out of bed. I let myself sink back down. A minute

later she returned with a porcelain bowl dating from the time when packages were delivered by the Pony Express, not FedEx. The edges were decorated with cows, haystacks, and cheerful peasants.

"I'm not hungry," I said.

American Buffalo clucked her tongue.

She held a spoon brimming with soup in front of my face so long and so patiently that I finally opened my lips a tiny bit. After swallowing that first spoonful I realized how hungry I was. I hadn't eaten a thing since our descent down the side of the office building, and I hadn't eaten the meal Vorkuta cooked up before we bombed the billboard. I'd been afraid of barfing it all up while I dangled above the street.

I took the spoon from American Buffalo's fingers and lapped up the soup until it was gone.

My hands were trembling a lot worse than hers.

I said I needed to go to the bathroom. There wasn't much light. I don't get why old people live in constant gloom. Are they preparing for the grave? I passed a full-length mirror and noticed I wasn't wearing anything but my panties. I asked for my jeans. American Buffalo nodded at the bathroom, where they were hanging above the tub. The tap didn't work, but there were two pails in there full of water. American Buffalo must have had a secret well where she drew her water. The cast-iron tub had heavy clawed feet; it looked like it had marched in from some elephant graveyard on the African savanna. On a shelf above the tub there was a row of brown glass bottles. They had white labels on them marked with Latin words, just like the jars they used to keep medicine in back before the steam engine was invented.

I had entered a world that had ceased to exist a hundred years earlier.

My shoes were leaning against the tub. Watery blood trickled from my wet jeans to the bottom of the tub and down the drain.

"Did I make a big mess?" I asked.

American Buffalo clucked her tongue again.

Evidently she took off her scarf inside her apartment. She wore her silver-gray hair in a long braid that reached halfway down her back.

"I didn't do anything," I protested, like a kid who's been caught breaking a window.

American Buffalo waved me back to bed. When I was lying down she unwrapped the bloody bandage from my left ankle and pressed her cold fingers into my leg. I howled and instinctively tried to kick. But she held my foot in a viselike grip, probing at the spaces between the tendons, bones, and muscles.

"They took an X-ray," I managed to say, as the tears welled up in my eyes.

American Buffalo clucked at me. Apparently it was her way of expressing both approval and disapproval. This sounded like the latter. She didn't seem to have much regard for X-rays and other medical tomfoolery invented since Columbus crossed the seas.

She had brought in one of the brown bottles from the bathroom. She dipped in her fingers and spread a thick layer of lemon-yellow ointment at two spots on my ankle. It smelled like rotten eggs and burned so badly I was sure it would eat through my skin.

"Owww! Goddammit!" I shouted.

"Tsk tsk tsk."

I didn't see how she could touch the stuff without gloves. I balled up the crocheted bedspread as I writhed in agony. I wanted to jump up, limp into the bathroom, and rinse off my leg. But American Buffalo wasn't having it. With her firm touch she had wrapped my ankle in a tight dressing that prevented me from getting at the ointment. The gauze she used was yellow with age.

"Where did you get that gauze?" I gasped. "The Napoleonic Wars? Were you one of those barbers who hacked off legs with a rusty saw?"

An aborted wheeze escaped American Buffalo's lips. In her emotive repertoire, this must have been her version of a rollicking laugh.

She hunched over to put the finishing touches on the dressing, and her long braid swung hypnotically in front of me. I held out my hand to touch it.

"You have beautiful hair," I said as I began to stroke it.

American Buffalo grunted and disappeared. She clattered around the kitchen and came back with a cup of tea that had so much honey stirred in it made my teeth ache. In her other hand, she held an old leather photo album. She opened it and flipped past pages of men in black suits and women in black skirts, chins raised and staring dead into the camera. The children in the photos looked like wax-figure miniatures of the grim adults, just as somber and world-weary by the age of five.

American Buffalo found what she was looking for. She turned the album around and put it in my hands. It was a portrait of a young man in uniform; he casually leaned against his sword, as if it were a walking stick. His boots gleamed like a mirror, and the tips of his whiskers narrowed to such sharp points that in a pinch they could have served as bayonets.

Next to him stood a woman who came up to his shoulders. She was trying to hold back her laughter; you could see the deep dimples in her cheeks. The thing that caught my attention was the woman's braid; it was so long it reached below her waist. The end of the braid and the bow of ribbon tying it off brushed against the mane of a rocking horse that stood between the couple.

A girl was sitting on the rocking horse.

"You?" I asked American Buffalo, pointing at the woman with the braid.

American Buffalo huffed and stabbed her clawlike forefinger at the little girl with the pigtails.

"You're the little girl?" I asked.

American Buffalo nodded. She went into the other room and retrieved a long, cinnamon-colored wooden box with brass hinges. She opened the lid. I could make out something thick and snakelike inside. She reached in and gingerly pulled out a braid almost as long as she was tall. She placed the braid in my hands as if it were a crystal goblet. The braid was thick, raven black, and glossy. There was no way you could Photoshop hair this perfect.

American Buffalo swung her gray braid out from behind her back and laid it next to the black braid. Shaking her head, she stroked her mother's braid, touched two fingers to her heart, and bit her lower lip.

"How old was your mother when she died?" I asked.

"Your age. I was a child. It was in this same bed. I pulled the blanket up to her chin. In the evening she coughed. In the morning she was dead."

American Buffalo sighed and tucked me in.

THE SCORPION'S NEST

All night long I listened to the cuckoo clock and the tinkle of the wind through the ventilation duct above my head. I didn't climb out of bed until the choppy snores from the next room came at a steady pace. The clock had just cuckooed four times.

I left a tuft of curly hair in the hollow of my pillow as a sign of gratitude.

I didn't dare use the crutches because of the noise they would make. I slowly dragged myself across the floor. The light in the corridor had burned out. I fumbled my way toward the stairwell, hugging the wall like a mouse. My ankle was still tender, but the constant throb wasn't permeating my body anymore, thanks to American Buffalo's ointment.

I wanted to get the hell out of that building, haul ass down the street, and disappear into the horizon on my crutches without ever looking back. But I couldn't. There was something I had to take care of first.

The summer dawn was breaking. In the pale light, I could see that Smew's and Alyosha's contorted bodies no longer sprawled at the bottom of the shaft. Someone had cleaned them up.

I turned on my headlamp before I stepped off the beam. I had switched out the batteries for ones I had found in an alarm clock on my nightstand at American Buffalo's place. I couldn't figure out why she needed an alarm clock: her cuckoo clock expressed itself so explosively every hour that I was constantly on edge.

The headlamp turned out to be unnecessary inside the Ice Cave. The cardboard had been torn down from almost all the windows. The attic was bathed in the pallid glow of streetlamps; the place looked ghostlier than it had in the pitch-black darkness.

The bloody footprints on the floor had disappeared, and the stench of cleaning supplies hung in the air. The smell was presumably supposed to make you think of a pine forest, but it put me back on the winding, nauseating roads of my childhood, with an air freshener swinging from the rearview mirror of a car that didn't have air conditioning.

The pools of blood had been soaked up and wiped away. The only sign they had ever existed was the odd blood-drunk bee crashing into the traffic signs.

The smashed computers had been carted off.

The trunk I had slept in was open.

I went into the laundry room. Both my mattress and Smew's mattress were gone. So were our backpacks. Mine didn't have any tags or anything that could be used to identify me. My hand instinctively slipped under my shirt, where I always carried my personal papers in a slim fabric pouch.

I stepped through the missing wall and into the main part of the attic. Alyosha's and Vorkuta's beds and belongings were also gone. Same with all the cans of spray paint, stencils, stickers, jars of paste, scissors, and carpet knives. Smew's camera was also gone.

Almost every trace of the Ice Rats had vanished. We no longer existed. The attic looked as if it had been twenty years since anyone had set foot in there.

I noticed gaps in the row of traffic signs leaning against the wall; even some of the signs were missing. The remaining ones alerted the traveler to numerous perils on his journey: deer, aircraft, tunnels, steep slopes, sheer drops.

I went back to the corner where the puddle of blood no longer was. I grabbed the traffic sign warning against tumbling rocks and moved it aside. There was another sign behind it, cautioning drivers as to the presence of children. I moved that, too.

Even the chairs had been removed, so I had to heap loose bricks into a jury-rigged step stool. I teetered at the top of the pile on my good foot and reached into a hollow in the wall. There was a gap in the bricks there, like a nest where scorpions lurk. After groping around for a moment my hand struck on a little recorder. I opened up the case and removed the memory card.

Just then I heard scratching behind me. I backed into the corner, but it only took me a second to realize that I'd be easy to spot in the deathly glow of the streetlamps. I limped over to the entrance, and when a figure in a black ski mask appeared I brought the CAUTION: CHILDREN sign down on the intruder's skull as hard as I could. The head slumped; I heard teeth clack. I flung the sign to the floor.

I dragged the black-clad body into the attic and peered out through the entrance. There was no one else on the beam. I pulled off the ski mask. The skin at the back of the scalp was broken; a bruise was already forming there.

The jacket had hiked up at the waist, revealing a strip of skin with three spines running up it.

THE DRAWBRIDGE

Vorkuta blinked. He instantly tried to bolt, but all he did was strain himself. I had lashed his upper body to one of the wooden support beams with a power cord. He had been out for a couple of hours and I was starting to worry I had whacked him too hard.

"You're tied to the stake. Prepare to be tortured by the natives," I said.

Vorkuta shook his head. "Goddammit, Metro, knock it off."

"Why did you kill them?"

"I could ask you the same thing."

Our squabbling intensified. Eventually my voice broke; my body was wracked by coughs. Vorkuta's cheeks were blazing.

"I don't believe you," I said.

"And I don't believe you."

"You're the one who's tied up."

"That doesn't make you the one telling the truth."

"I could kill you," I growled.

"I'm sure you could. You have a reputation for killing the wrong people."

"Shut your hole." I gave the wooden beam above Vorkuta's head a solid wallop with my crutch.

"Missed," Vorkuta said. "Aim better if you want to kill me the way you killed my boyfriend."

I saw the tears well up in Vorkuta's eyes and realized what he had just said. They had been a couple.

Back in Pripyat, Vorkuta and Alyosha had squatted in the same building as Smew and me. There had originally been a third Russian guy in our crew, but he had taken off at some point.

At first, while I was painting my mural for Rust, Vorkuta and Smew shared an apartment. When I finished the piece, Smew and I moved into a place that had a view of the reactor, and Vorkuta and Alyosha had taken over a flat on the top floor of our sixteen-story building. I thought they did it because, in the long run, it was more fun bunking with someone else than living alone in the abandoned city.

Alyosha and Vorkuta hung out together all the time, shoving each other and ruffling each other's hair, but I'd just assumed they were friends. Kind of like me and Smew. The two of us had slept most nights in the same room since we'd left Finland. We had smelled each other's damp, sweaty clothes and dirty hair, at first in Chernobyl and now in Berlin. But it had never occurred to me that anyone would think we were together.

"So you guys were a couple," I mumbled. "A real couple."

"I'm sure it was pretty hard to notice since you couldn't shut up about Rust the Divine. 'Ooh, amazing Rust. He was perfect, so charming, he drove me crazy, his broad shoulders, his firm jaw, so incredibly handsome, my prince, my Hercules, my Hollywood hero Rust.' Because no one else in this world would be capable of true love except you and your pearl-crusted, myrrh-scented Rust. Did he even use the bathroom? Of course not. Gods don't produce any waste. Everything that touches their lips turns to pure energy. Did he even have an asshole?"

I gulped. My throat was dry. "That's not true."

Vorkuta let out a metallic guffaw; blood dripped from his mouth and nose. His laugh looked as horrible as it sounded.

"So, you guys had a fight, you and Alyosha?" I said. "You lost your temper and killed him?"

"Yeah, you're exactly right. It was a crime of passion," Vorkuta spat out. "You probably planned on killing Rust the Divine every time you argued over whose turn it was to clean. Or when Rust left his tooth-brush in the wrong spot. Or when he snored at night. You decided then and there you'd bash Rust's head in and kill a few of his friends while you were at it. And then come back later to clean up the place."

I sat down next to Vorkuta and leaned against the wooden pillar.

"The Banksy is gone," I said, giving Vorkuta a quick glance.

"I did that, too. I carried it out on my back."

"How did they get the wall out in one piece?"

"They lifted it through the roof. They cut a big hole in the metal sheeting and hoisted it out."

"What the hell are you talking about?" I said, looking up. "The roof's right where it always was."

"If you untie me I'll show you. I can't show you anything with my arms tied."

I closed my eyes; my head was buzzing. What if Vorkuta was jealous of Smew? What if Alyosha and Smew had fallen in love with each other and Vorkuta caught them messing around and got rid of both of them? There was one problem with this equation. Smew was as passionate as a wet rag. I'd never seen Smew fall in love with anything except dusty, junk-filled abandoned buildings. We used to laugh about it back in Kotka, joke that the day Smew's mom demanded he get married and start a family, the bride he'd drag to the altar would be some dilapi-dated cabin he'd discovered deep in the woods. Or a witch's cottage, like from "Hansel and Gretel." In Pripyat and here in Berlin, I'd undressed in front of him and changed clothes and pranced around half-naked. Smew never stared or turned away in fake modesty; he just kept at whatever he was doing. He wasn't interested in tits and ass. I hadn't remembered him checking out guys, either. It was more like he shied from any touch. Unless the secret object of his passion was a rusted anvil he stumbled across in an abandoned smithy, or a wall half-eaten by rot. Those were the kinds of things he would occasionally stroke.

"Hel-lo," Vorkuta called out. "Did you bite the dust, too?"

I shook myself out of my reverie and unwrapped the power cord from around Vorkuta. It had dug deeply into his arms, but he didn't complain. He straightened out his legs, then he picked up the traffic sign I had brained him with. He took a step toward me. For a second I thought, *Now he's going to get back at me, split my skull.* He had heavy hands powerful enough to swing a sledgehammer all day. But he stepped past me and toward the missing wall. He held the traffic sign up by its post and jabbed at the ceiling. The sheet of metal roofing overhead rose. A strip of early-morning sky the width of a wall appeared above us.

"How?"

"They brought in a mobile crane with a boom that was taller than the building."

"I saw the truck that carried off the Banksy. It was a robbery."

"What make?"

"I'm not sure. A truck."

"What was the license plate number?"

"I didn't look."

"Don't you remember anything at all about it?"

"It had a white cab. I think."

"You're a piece of work," Vorkuta said with a sigh. "Would you notice if war broke out on the next block over?"

"I was focused on something else."

"You were focused on shoving your head up your ass."

Vorkuta told me he came across the scene of the murders earlier than I did, around 5:00 a.m., while I was still dozing on the bench at the doctor's. Alyosha had texted him from there. Vorkuta was still at

Museum Island then; he had spent the night poking around the place. One of his biggest dreams was doing some serious graffiti there. The walls were full of surveillance cameras; there was probably a higher concentration of them there than anywhere else in Berlin, and he had been looking for a good spot to do some work. Another one of his dreams was to do a big piece on the wall of the Russian embassy. Plenty of surveillance cameras there, too, plus armed guards.

"I hung around the island for about an hour after Alyosha texted me," Vorkuta said. "I found a couple of decent spots. When I got back here the electricity was off. I had a flashlight with me and I saw the blood and the smashed computers. Then I noticed the roof had been peeled back. The stars were shining overhead and a satellite happened to orbit past while I was looking up."

"So there was a hole in the roof then? There wasn't one when I was here."

"As I was wondering what the hell was going on, the crane lowered the roofing back into place," Vorkuta said.

He told me he didn't waste any time; he bailed as soon as he realized that whoever had found the Ice Cave was still around. He almost lost his footing on the beam when he saw the two bodies down below.

"That's when I knew it was Russian homophobes who had paid us a visit. We used to get death threats from them back in Russia."

"Huh?"

"Yeah, either that or the FSB."

"The what?"

"The Russian security service. The successor to the KGB. Or the FSB has shopped out the job to foreign intelligence, the SVR."

"Come on, you don't have to get crazy."

"They're after Alyosha and me. It's all the same organization. We've managed to hide from them until now, but it looks like they've caught up to us. They haven't forgiven us for painting a boner that could be seen from the headquarters of the secret police."

"What the hell?"

"On a drawbridge that crosses the Neva River. Whenever that side of the bridge went up, a seventy-meter penis would point straight at the windows of the FSB. Up and down. Up and down. Those dicks had to stare at a fat, juicy dick day and night."

"You're lying."

"I wish I were. And it wasn't the only piece we did. But it's the one we got caught for. They found out our names."

I was at a loss for words. I had never imagined him as some queer activist who went around painting giant dicks as eye candy for the Russian secret police. I always thought he was a shy country boy, like Smew, the kind of guy who lives with his mom forever and never gets his shit together enough to move out on his own. When you had your mother looking after you, you were solid for food and clean underwear.

Vorkuta said he belonged to a crew that defended the rights of homosexuals. They painted in major Russian cities, choosing the most prominent spots possible and disseminating their work online. Two people from the crew had been arrested for the drawbridge scandal, and Alyosha and Vorkuta had checked out and headed for Pripyat for the first time. They would return there when things got too hot in the metropolis.

"OK, so now we're on the hit list of the FSB. And the TVH, and the ABC, and however many more of those three-letter acronyms there are."

"It's not like you did anything," Vorkuta said, trying to quiet my fear.

"Where else did you paint besides that drawbridge?"

"Oh, around," Vorkuta mumbled.

"Like where?"

"The walls of the Kremlin."

"What? Fuck me."

"A rainbow. And a little message."

"What little message?"

"Mr. President! Come out of the closet! Join us!"

"When?"

"Right before we left for Pripyat in the spring. We uploaded some photos of it, too. Putin's been busy trying to scrub them from the Net."

"OK. There's no way this can get any worse," I said.

"We went and posed naked in front of it wearing ski masks. Apparently the FSB has measured the dick lengths of gay Russians, called in urologists and conducted all kinds of image analysis, calculated how much the freezing temperatures that night affected length and girth."

"TMI," I said, curling up in a ball on the floor.

I was still too shocked to comprehend how my life had suddenly turned into a nightmare. In Pripyat, we'd been allowed to relive our lost childhoods for weeks on end. I'd painted all day long. You had to keep an eye out for the camera-wielding tour groups drawn by the radioactive area, but they weren't too much trouble. The same with the first weeks in Berlin. For the most part, it was like free admission to a circus that was open 24/7. From time to time Verboten had tapped us for mandatory rent-payment jobs, but I'd had plenty of time to work on my own graffiti without constantly worrying about being chased by growling Rottweilerish guards. They hadn't existed in Pripyat, and in Berlin people were more open-minded about tags and pieces than they had been in Finland.

I hadn't realized I was living with a time bomb. Two time bombs: Alyosha and Vorkuta. Two activists the Russian government was hunting down for hooliganism and terrorism and god knows what antistate anarchism. In Pripyat they had seemed like two harmless hippies whose most vigorous form of activism was bickering loudly about the best recipe for cooking mushrooms.

Couldn't the rest of the crew be more like me, goddammit? Well-balanced people who had their shit together?

I lay there for what felt like hours as confused thoughts ricocheted around my skull. Vorkuta sat quietly at my side for a while, then he started clearing his throat and pacing back and forth across the attic. When I still didn't move, he tapped me on the shoulder.

"You don't have to worry. They have a lot of other suspects, too," he said. "We're going to get through this. Let's take it easy. Count to ten."

I only made it to six before an earth-shattering crash boomed out from the left wall, and the whole floor of the attic tipped up. Before my eyes, Vorkuta started sliding toward a hole that had appeared in the wall.

PEAR OF STEEL

Vorkuta successfully lunged for the support beam, but during the next shudder I lost my grip and slid across the slippery, just-scrubbed floor. My crutches clattered away.

Vorkuta crawled over on his hands and knees and grabbed my shoulder. He dragged me along the floor and over to the fat beam, told me to hold on with both hands.

"My crutches!" I said, gasping. "I need my crutches."

One of my crutches was caught in some loose bricks, but the other had scudded toward the hole that had appeared at the bottom of the wall. It teetered there at the edge.

"Hold on," Vorkuta said.

He crawled over and retrieved the nearest crutch first. He was on his way to rescue the second one when another deep boom thundered in front of us, echoing through the walls. The attic shook. A crack appeared in the beam I was hugging; the wood split into a grinning mouth.

The second crash hurled Vorkuta headfirst toward the edge of the hole. He managed to steady his foot against a warped window frame and spring up the tilted floor, but he lost his grip on the crutch. It fell. Vorkuta clambered over to me.

"We have to get out of here," he said.

"What is it?"

"Demo crew."

"Demolition wasn't supposed to happen for months!"

"Tell *them*."

Vorkuta snatched a signpost and stabbed at the loose sheet of roofing. It popped to the side, revealing a gap a couple of palm widths wide.

"Hold this up," Vorkuta ordered.

The post was just long enough; the triangular tip of the sign scratched against the edge of the metal roof.

Something beyond the wall boomed again, knocking me to my knees. A flock of startled swifts appeared, flitting and flying wildly among the beams.

Vorkuta dragged over one of the smashed monitors. He grabbed the signpost from me and jammed it inside the monitor.

"Footing," he explained. "So it'll stay in place."

Vorkuta staggered over to get a second monitor and another traffic sign; this one warned against slippery roads instead of children. The floor was quaking the whole time; bits of wood, bird's nests, eggshells, skeletons of long-dead pigeons, dust, and rubble showered down on us from above. The swifts screeched and beat their wings. The apartment building was heaving in its death throes.

I didn't understand how Vorkuta was still standing. I had been on my ass the whole time, watching out for my injured foot.

"It's a ladder," Vorkuta said. "You first."

I gripped the signposts and wrapped my legs around them. Vorkuta gave me a boost, and after struggling for what seemed like forever I reached the top. I nudged aside the piece of metal sheeting with my head and shoulders and wriggled onto the roof through the small gap.

I lay there facedown, holding the traffic signs steady from the top. I could see pieces of the building's outer walls raining down behind Vorkuta. It was like a dream the instant before you wake up: the walls collapsing around you and the ground sliding out from under you as the world you know comes to an end.

"My crutch!" I shouted. "I need it."

"Goddammit, Metro!"

Vorkuta chucked the crutch up. I pulled my head back just in time; otherwise it would have whacked me in the face. I clenched it between my knees so I wouldn't lose it. I steadied the signposts as Vorkuta hoisted himself up through the hole and onto the roof. He panted there at my side as the roof boomed repeatedly. We watched the three-by-five-meter piece of metal sheeting slide down the sloped surface and disappear over the edge.

"What the fuck is happening?" I asked.

"Wrecking ball," Vorkuta said, "swinging from the crane that hoisted out the Banksy."

We slithered to the other side of the roof on our bellies and made for the next building. I could feel the Ice Cave writhe beneath me; metal gutters and eaves plunged into oblivion. I felt something on my calf. I glanced over my shoulder. A family of rats—actual rats—was scurrying across my legs, following the roofline; they were headed in the same direction we were. The next building over was their lifeboat, too.

The adjacent old warehouse was taller than our building by about a meter, and a two-meter gap separated the two structures. The rat family hustled across the gap on electric wiring; even the tiniest ones knew to balance themselves with their tails as they scampered across. I looked down; it was twenty meters to the ground. The wires wouldn't take the weight of a cat, let alone a human.

"Is there a ladder around somewhere?" I shouted.

"In the collapsed section of the building."

We were lying there at the peak of the roof, side by side, as the wrecking ball appeared above the roof line. Somewhere down below in his cab, an invisible operator let the ball crash through the roof into the attic. Over and over. The wrecking ball was pummeling our Ice Cave to bits.

"Should we show ourselves?" I said.

"We're definitely done for, then."

"It could be a mistake. Maybe they don't know we're here."

"Wait here," Vorkuta said, backing up and disappearing behind a ventilation duct. Metal sheeting squealed, bricks rattled, beams and walls splintered. I was lying on a sheet-metal ice floe that was shrinking by the minute.

I could have sworn I heard someone crying for help.

I pricked up my ears. Vorkuta was calling to me amid the racket.

I retraced my path along the roof line. The wrecking ball's blows had punched an enormous hole in the roof, providing a clear view several stories down. The floor to the attic no longer existed. Vorkuta was bending back the sheet metal at the edge of the hole.

"Are you fucking deaf?" he hissed. "Grab the other end."

A long strip of metal sheeting was halfway off. We yanked at it until the nails popped. The edge was razor sharp; I stretched the sleeves of my leather coat over my palms so I wouldn't cut my hands. We finally managed to loosen the piece of sheeting; it was a lot taller than we were.

"This might be enough," Vorkuta said.

"You gotta be fucking kidding me."

"Do you have a better idea? If you do, now is the time to say so."

A powerful crash rocked through our bodies. The building staggered beneath us, as if one of its vertebrae had snapped. The wrecking ball was swinging from the courtyard toward the inner wall again. The roof in front of us pitched up more steeply.

So much for talk. We dragged our sheet of metal roofing toward the end of the building facing the warehouse. The wall there was still standing, and we maneuvered our sheeting so it formed a slanted bridge between the two roofs. The sheet bounced up and down and it was hard to find a spot where we could put it over the space between buildings. It had to be held firmly in place; otherwise it would slide down from the bucking roof.

"Go," Vorkuta said.

"No, you."

"I'll hold on."

There was no time to argue. The building shivered. I unsteadily scrambled up and across the slanted surface; it was like trying to cross the drawbridge over the Neva that Vorkuta had told me about. I kept expecting it to pop up completely vertical.

A rat ran across my back; its claws scratched my neck.

Another rat family was fleeing. They made it to the roof of the warehouse before I did.

Now it was my turn to hold the metal against the edge of the roof. Vorkuta started climbing across. The sheeting lurched as the roof behind him danced. I remembered the time we went to the science center when I was a kid; they had a spring-loaded floor that was supposed to mimic an earthquake. We had all laughed and bumped into each other on purpose.

No one was laughing now.

I could see the wrecking ball pick up speed in the courtyard.

Vorkuta lunged for my crutch with one hand. He hung on as the crutch crushed me against the roof. Our metal bridge bounced and crashed somewhere far below. Vorkuta hurled himself up to the warehouse. We crawled on.

Behind a chimney, we found a hatch that the chimney sweeps and satellite-dish installers used for roof access. Vorkuta booted the edge of the hatch and beat it with my crutch so long that the hinge on the inside eventually came loose. We dropped in, descended the warehouse's cast-iron stairways past deserted corridors. One floor smelled faintly of coffee, another sharply of piss. We climbed out through a small first-floor window that we forced open from the inside. The street was teeming with curious neighbors so we slipped in among the crowd.

The street was closed off at both ends, and barriers had been put up around the crane. Big men in overalls stood inside the barriers; someone in the courtyard was guiding the pear-shaped steel ball that swung through the air, crushing our home to chunks of concrete, brick, and glass. The top two floors had already disappeared.

With every swing, a cloud erupted into the air as water was sprayed from a nearby tanker truck in a futile effort to minimize the amount of dust everywhere.

"We have to get out of here," Vorkuta said.

"Wait."

I had noticed American Buffalo. She was hunched over right next to the barrier, watching her home vanish. Underneath her was the same chair she'd been sitting on when she bound my ankle. She was staring at the broken windows without batting an eye, at the fragments and motes of wood that rained to the ground all up and down the block.

Her belongings had been chucked into the bed of a truck; the asphalt was littered with broken brown glass. An irritated-looking guy in a suit was trying to hustle American Buffalo into the passenger seat. In her arms she clutched a long wooden box the color of cinnamon.

SAMUEL

I watched from the shelter of the sausage stand as Dad stepped off the train, as dejected as last time, drank his cup of coffee, and trudged home. I waited until I saw the bluish light flicker on inside his apartment.

Vorkuta was next to me, counting the stars or the streetlamps. I nudged him in the ribs. We slipped in on the heels of the next person to enter Dad's building, nodded good evening.

I rang Dad's doorbell.

The apartment was silent. The peephole went dark; someone was looking out at us. The silence continued.

I rang the doorbell again.

The television was turned up louder.

"You and your dad have a good relationship, huh?" Vorkuta asked.

I kicked the door several times.

"It's Maria," I shouted right into the peephole. "Your daughter!"

Silence.

"So your name's Maria," Vorkuta said.

"You can forget you ever heard that. I'm always Metro to you."

The door opened a finger's width, and a familiar-looking eye peered out.

"We need a place to sleep," I said.

"I don't really have the room here right now," Dad said and grunted.

I forced my way in. "You live here by yourself, goddammit. I know you do."

I made a right turn into the room that gave off the ghostly blue ambience I'd seen from across the street. There, on a small stool in front of the television, sat a young boy. He was glued to a cartoon of a cat flying through the air and splashing into water. He was laughing.

"Yes," said Dad from behind me, clearing his throat, "it's my turn to take care of Samuel."

I was stunned. "This is your kid? Who's the mother? Where is she? What the hell have you done?"

Dad shook his head and disappeared into the kitchenette, where he started clattering around. I settled onto the carpet next to the boy. Now the cat was in a rowboat missing the plug. He was trying to row and bail the boat at the same time and ended up at the bottom, staring an octopus in the eye.

Smew wouldn't have liked this. He was more afraid of water than anything else.

He didn't need to be afraid of anything anymore.

But the little boy was giggling at the cat's persistent attempts to make it to the island in the middle of the lake.

His giggles were infectious. I found myself smiling. Dad brought us cups of cocoa. Vorkuta had curled up on the sofa in front of the window, trying to camouflage himself among the pillows.

"I didn't think I would ever see you again," Dad said.

"Well, here I am."

"Do you live in Berlin?"

"It's a long story. We need a place to crash for a few nights. We lost our home."

"You couldn't make rent?"

"That's one way of putting it."

Dad sighed. He eyed Vorkuta and me, and then he took a seat at the other end of the sofa.

"Your boyfriend?"

"Yeah. His name is Vorkuta."

"Vorkuta is the name of a prison camp, not a person," Dad said.

"What?" I said. "What are you talking about?"

I glanced over at Vorkuta. He shook his head.

"You never answered my postcards," Dad said.

"I'm here now. Where's Samuel's mother?"

"Samuel doesn't have a mother."

"Of course not. Is there any woman in this world you're capable of living with?"

"Samuel's mother is dead."

"You just said it was your turn to watch him. You're lying. Where's Samuel while you're at work?"

"The neighbor watches him. She has a child who's the same age. Samuel's mother really is dead. You've always had a hard time accepting the truth, Maria. Even when you were a child."

I bit my lip and slurped my cocoa. Dad lowered his hand to my shoulder; I shrugged it off. He sighed, stood, and told Samuel it was time for bed. Samuel shook his head, wiggled his toes, and snickered at the stars orbiting above the huge lump on the cartoon cat's head.

Later that night, Dad came back into the living room. Vorkuta had taken throw pillows and a blanket from the couch and crashed on the bathroom floor. The light from the streetlamps bothered him; he was used to sleeping in the darkness.

I was watching, for what was probably the fifteenth time, fuzzy footage of three men. The picture from the surveillance camera Smew had set up was a blur. The men's faces melted into a dark paste because they were wearing something over their faces.

Dad took a seat. I paused the recording.

"Who are they?" he asked. "Your friends?"

"Far from it."

"Have you gotten yourself into some sort of trouble?"

"I haven't done anything," I mumbled. "I just need a roof over my head for a couple of nights." I fiddled with the remote in agitation, waiting for Dad to leave. When he didn't budge, I said, "You and your son have the same name."

"You like it?"

"Samuel Sr. and Samuel Jr. Sounds just like America."

"In my family, we pass down names from one generation to the next. The oldest son has been named Samuel for many generations."

"Girls don't matter, I guess."

"My mother's name was Maria," Dad said. "Maria was a good woman, the bravest one I've ever known."

"How's she doing? Do you send a card to her in the Congo once a year, the way you used to send me one in Finland?"

"Some men who attacked our house killed Maria when I was seven. She managed to hide me in the brush."

I had a hard time thinking of a snappy retort to this. We sat silently on the sofa side by side. The paused image crackled.

"I have work in the morning," Dad finally said.

"I can watch Samuel."

"Nothing must happen to him."

"Why would anything happen to him?" I cried.

Dad shushed me. A drowsy voice called from the bedroom, which is where Dad headed after telling me to get to bed.

I sat there in the darkness, rewinding the recording over and over. Yet again, three men crossed the span toward the Ice Cave. I recognized one of them as Verboten, despite the scarf pulled up over his face. I could tell by the way he moved along the beam. He didn't know about the hidden camera; Smew and I were the only ones who did. Verboten would have flipped if he had found out about it. Among writers, surveillance cameras are a more despised technology than nuclear warheads. Smew had cobbled together a recording system; a motion sensor automatically turned on the camera anytime it detected movement on the beam. Smew had been nervous about the junkies living downstairs. He'd been afraid that they would enter the Ice Cave and take anything they could carry. It wouldn't be hard to find the key to the steel door hanging under the stairs, and all you had to do at the other end was move aside the camouflaged plywood if you knew what lay behind it. *This is between you and me,* Smew had said as he concealed the wiring. I had felt so shitty about it, like I was a security guard or something. I had decided I wouldn't tell the others about it. I had also decided I would never watch the footage it recorded. Ever.

But here I was, watching it.

In the recording, Verboten was entering the Ice Cave, followed by two guys. They were both burlier than Verboten, clumsier on the beam.

The image went dark; Smew's system worked on some sort of timer. If the motion sensor didn't get a signal within about a minute, the camera turned off.

The image came back, and there was Verboten exiting the Ice Cave. Alone.

The image went dark again.

Then the television screen showed the two burly guys in masks coming out of the Ice Cave, backs hunched. They were having a tough time moving. They were dragging two bodies, which they hurled from the beam. It was the easiest way of getting the bodies to the bottom.

I paused the footage at the point when the second body was being dropped. It was Smew; his face was still intact, and I could make out the Secundas T-shirt.

"Fuck," I muttered.

Vorkuta's snores echoed from the little bathroom. He had watched the recording twice before leaving the room. He couldn't stand to watch Alyosha being dropped over and over again.

I sat there in the darkness, transfixed by Smew's and Alyosha's final moments. Over and over. From time to time, I wiped my eyes.

THE PUZZLE

The days that followed were the happiest I'd had in a long time. After the first night, Vorkuta checked out of Dad's apartment, saying it would be safer if we didn't sleep in the same place. He told me I wouldn't be any use with a bum foot. The best thing I could do was concentrate on getting in shape.

"I want to come," I said.

"You won't be able to keep up. I have a couple of ideas."

So I took my half brother to the park every day. He barely raised an eyebrow when he heard I was his sister. Dad had told him that his sister was a sailor who was on a voyage around the world. She had frolicked on tropical islands, climbed the Himalayas, and bicycled along the Great Wall of China. It was no big deal when she showed up at a one-bedroom flat in Friedrichshain one day.

I pushed Samuel in the swing until my arms were sore.

We kicked around the soccer ball. He liked sending it in the wrong direction so I would have to chase after it. But I didn't yell at him. I liked hearing the titters behind my back as I went into the bushes, looking for the ball.

He enthusiastically built teeny-tiny huts from dried pine needles and twigs and leaves and called me over to look at them. Then he'd stomp on the hut and mash it into the ground, growling in a low *Exorcist* voice: *Haaaa!*

But Samuel was no horror-movie brat. I could have watched him climb the sprawling structures at the playground until dark day in and day out. I grinned more times in a couple of hours than I remembered having smiled in months.

One day, he suddenly stopped climbing, scrambled down from the jungle gym, and ran up to me.

"Is the water warm?" he asked, staring at me with his big eyes.

"Where?"

"On your tropical island."

"Yup. It never gets cold there."

Samuel nodded solemnly, then he climbed back up the green structure that looked like some hybrid metal pine tree from a futuristic forest.

It was a hot day, and people licked ice cream cones as they walked past. I wished I could buy one for Samuel, but I didn't have any money. I scanned the ground. No coins, just bottle caps. Rust told me once that I had such long, narrow fingers I'd make a good pickpocket. Or piano player. Neither career ever materialized.

I suddenly lost my balance. I had bumped into Samuel. He had stepped out in front of me without my noticing and was staring at me again.

"Well, what is it?" I asked.

"Do you know how to swim?"

"Not very well. Why?"

"Out at the island. How did you get away if you don't know how to swim?"

"In a boat. I came the rest of the way by river."

"Where's the boat?"

"I'll show you someday."

He fell silent again, nodding seriously to himself. It was only my third day at Dad's, and I was already lying fluently to a four-year-old in my lousy German.

Spending time with my half brother somehow distracted me; I wasn't constantly preoccupied by what happened to Smew and Alyosha. As I kept watching the surveillance camera recording, the idea of going to the police occurred to me, contrary to all my instincts. But during what must have been about the thirtieth viewing I realized that wouldn't make any sense. We'd been squatting in an attic; officially we hadn't even been there. Two murders had been committed, but the bodies had in all likelihood been disposed of. A work of art by Banksy had been stolen. *Oh, really? Which one?* The only people who knew of its existence were the squatters and the thieves. I hadn't ID'd the truck properly. The only solid piece of evidence was the recorded footage, in which two unidentified, blurry-faced men dropped two other unidentified, equally blurry-faced men from a steel beam. But there was no way of telling whether the drop was half a meter or twenty meters. There was no air of violence about what was seen on the screen. The footage, which lasted only for a few seconds, looked more like friends wrestling on some boom.

To outside eyes, my proof was as intangible as rustling wind in tall grass. The police would probably be less interested in my story than they were in me. And Vorkuta. And how the fuck did it just so happen that the building where I claimed the murders had taken place had been demolished in the meantime? If I didn't end up in jail, I'd end up in the loony bin, cooling my jets and coming down from my delusions.

That evening the three of us had pizza for dinner. Dad picked up two Margherita pizzas from the joint on the corner where a plastic pie glowed red and yellow above the door, looking like one of the traffic signs from the Ice Cave. As I munched on my slices, I explained how if you wanted to make money you needed to forget about running one measly little pizzeria. Instead, you had to focus on manufacturing the cardboard boxes in which pizzas were carried out from the thousands and thousands of local pizzerias struggling to break even. If I wanted to make a fortune, I'd buy a cardboard factory that manufactured pizza boxes, and I'd also make cardboard boxes in other custom sizes. Nowadays grocery stores sell cardboard packaging in greater quantities than food that's been packed in it. A surefire recipe for success: don't invest in content, invest in packaging.

Samuel glanced at me over his slice; the tomato sauce had stained his nose and the corners of his mouth. He sank his teeth greedily back into his dinner. Dad sat there staring at me for a moment, then he shook his head and continued eating.

"You were terribly feisty, even as a child," Dad said.

"No, I wasn't."

"I remember one summer that was so hot, and all you wanted to do was wear your rubber boots. No rain for weeks. Broiling hot. The sun was shining the whole time. The other kids were running around barefoot. But you wore your rubber boots. One time your mother and I hid them, and you shrieked for hours, demanding they be returned to you. Then you held your breath so long you went beet red and veins were popping out of your forehead. We had to give you the boots back."

"They were orange," I mumbled. "They were cool."

"When it finally rained, after weeks of hot weather, you wanted to go barefoot."

"Of course. I didn't want my boots to get dirty."

Dad sighed. I converted my slice into an angry face; basil leaves were the slanted eyes, and a slice of tomato was the shouting mouth. Dad's sigh sounded exactly the same as I remembered it from childhood. Back then, I thought his sighing was Mom's fault, but maybe it was mine. Maybe they got divorced because I was one element too many in the equation.

"Have you ever considered making things easier on yourself?" Dad asked, switching to Finnish so Samuel wouldn't understand. "It doesn't always have to be you against the world."

"Why? So I end up like you?"

Dad didn't say anything, but he offered me another slice of pizza. We ate in silence for a bit longer.

"Maria, I'm sorry I left when I did," Dad said out of the blue. "I shouldn't have done that."

"I'm not Maria. I'm Metro."

"If I hadn't left I would have died in that country. It was too cold for me there, too dark, too colorless."

"You should have taken me with you."

"It's just as cold, dark, and colorless here. My problems don't originate from the place, but from me. Your mother and I weren't meant to be together."

"How so?"

"It would have been better if we had never met."

"Then I never would have been born."

"That's not what I meant."

"It's exactly what you meant. Goddammit! Decide already, Samuel Sr.! Was it a mistake I was born, or was it a mistake I turned out the way I did?"

Dad sighed, rose from the table, and shuffled over to the coffee table in the living room. Samuel glanced at me; he was covered in tomato sauce. His huge eyes contained a world of blame.

I didn't feel like eating anymore. Ending the staring contest with Samuel, I followed Dad into the living room. He had spread out a piece of cardboard on the coffee table. It looked like the unfolded remnants of some earlier pizza box, and it had a partially finished puzzle on it. The edges were in place, plus a few blobs from the middle. In the finished bits, you could see little people moving back and forth.

"Are you familiar with this?" Dad asked.

"No."

"It's the ceiling of the Sistine Chapel. Painted by Michelangelo."

"Graffiti, huh?"

"Well, yes, in a way."

Samuel walked up to the puzzle. Dad told him he had to wash his face and hands first.

"He's good at this. Watch," Dad said.

Samuel came back to the table. He hummed to himself and started putting together pieces that to my eyes looked completely identical.

"Where's the birdy's wing?" he said and hummed. "Here's the birdy's wing. Where's the birdy's foot? Here's the birdy's foot."

"It's an angel," I said.

"It's a birdy," Samuel said, snapping the piece into place.

"Where's the old man's toes? Here's the old man's toes," he continued, forming some ancient prophet with a long beard.

A shadow fell across my face. I glanced up; Dad had adjusted the floor lamp so it was aiming at the puzzle.

"Is this what you guys do at night?" I asked.

"Is there something wrong with doing puzzles?"

"No. I thought you guys just stared at the boob tube. Or that you stared at it alone."

"Where did you get that idea?" Dad said, his eyes narrowing. "Have you been watching us long?"

"Only once," I lied. "From the balcony of that building across the street. Just for a minute. I had to make sure you weren't some serial killer."

"Me? What world is it you live in, Maria?"

"A different one from yours."

I didn't mention that when I spied on him, I thought Dad was totally burnt out, spent, sapped of his love for life. Based on what I'd seen over the last couple of days, he seemed a lot more chipper than me.

I tried to mash a bit of scroll into place.

"Wrong," Samuel said immediately.

"No, it's not."

"Wrong!"

My next attempt also ended with being reprimanded by Samuel's bright voice. I satisfied myself with watching his tiny fingers pick up one piece after another, most of them upside down, and stitch them together as fast as a sewing machine. There was something mesmerizing about his movements. Gradually, the certainty crept into my mind that it would be possible to fit the pieces into their rightful places and restore order to the world.

"Samuel is going to be something someday," Dad said. "I want to give him that chance. I didn't give it to you, and I regret it."

Samuel handed me a piece that had a bit of flowing green robe. He pointed his forefinger at the spot where I was supposed to put it. The first attempt went awry; the second time, it fit.

"You'll learn," Samuel said, putting another piece in my hand. "Take your time. There's nothing to be afraid of."

I bit my lip. My eyes went dark, and the blood rushed in my ears. I didn't realize Dad had gotten up until he came back from the entryway and gestured at the door. I hadn't heard the doorbell ring. Vorkuta was standing there, holding his nose, which was dripping blood on the doormat. His jacket sleeve was shredded and blood was also beading up on a big scrape on his elbow.

"I found Verboten," he said.

THE GALLERY

Vorkuta had me stop at a traffic signal and nodded over at the other side of the street. An orange baby carriage was parked there. In front of it, a small, sharp-nosed dog was wrestling with a stack of windblown paper—and losing, badly.

"We came all this way to watch a miniature pooch get its ass kicked by a newspaper?" I asked.

"Look behind it."

There was a commercial space at the corner; Vorkuta walked me over to it. I leaned on my crutch just to play it safe, although by this point my foot could already take a little weight. The corner property's huge windows covered more surface area than the square footage of several studio apartments. Graffiti-covered butcher paper obscured the glass. I immediately recognized the artist. The writer's name had been written across the butcher paper in multiple languages:

VERBOTEN FORBIDDEN VIETATO PROHIBIDO

Before we got too close to the building Vorkuta pointed out a bug-eyed surveillance camera lurking overhead. In another meter or so we would step into range. Vorkuta pointed at the edge of the window. The butcher paper didn't reach all the way to the jamb.

We could see in through the crack.

It was an art gallery. The floor was covered in paint-splattered butcher paper with Verboten's name written across it, over and over again. The ceiling had been completely papered over in long strips cut from the same roll of brown paper. The wall served as a backdrop for traffic signs, some of which I recognized from the Ice Cave. Like the CROSSWALK sign; a tidal wave had been painted behind the figure crossing the street, on the verge of devouring him. The airplane on the AIRPORT sign was now approaching New York's Twin Towers.

The modifications were Smew's handiwork. One evening he'd been inspired to tweak the signs, decorating the Ice Cave with motifs taken from the news. Smew felt that the news was nothing but ads for catastrophes these days, and the reason for this was financial; it wasn't because our world was somehow more dangerous. Media outlets all over the world stayed afloat by creating new causes for alarm and panic. It was in the media's interest to keep humanity in a state of constant horror over some fresh disaster: bird flu, terrorists, Ebola. The media live off fear-mongering; keeping people in a state of dread increases the number of media consumers and, thereby, advertising income. The media and the advertisers walk arm in arm down this path, fanning the flames of panic and feeding off fright. The slew of security companies and other businesses built on people craving safety form the third tip of this triangle. They benefit from the impression that the world is awash in deadly diseases and deranged suicide bombers.

So Smew had started painting the traffic signs in the Ice Cave to reflect the current media climate. In their original form the signs were too neutral; every sign needed to be harnessed to bring people face-to-face with dire threat. On the CAMPGROUND sign he had painted flames licking at the tent and the RV; cars on a FREEWAY sign plunged into cracks and crevasses he had added to the lanes.

And now Smew's handiwork was covering one wall of the gallery. A video of our most recent train-painting job was projected on another wall, our life-size images moving across the surface. Even though my face was covered by a shemagh, I had no trouble recognizing myself. A hand emerged from the train and grabbed me, and I sprayed its owner in the eyes with ice-blue paint. The video ended with the camera turning to shoot the approaching security guards and dogs. Smew, who was the cameraman, had been running as he recorded; the lurching image showed the guards catching up to us. After a brief pause, big letters appeared on the wall—THE ICE RATS GNAW AT THE CITY—and the video started all over again.

Next to this video projection stood two real live humans in the flesh.

The first was Verboten; he was talking to a woman I'd never seen before who had purple hair and was wearing a skirt suit. They were examining a group of works Verboten had created: female figures with big tits, whose heads were televisions, irons, footballs. During our weeks in the Ice Cave I had never developed much of a taste for Verboten's motifs. As we prowled the city together, he confided that he was constantly searching for new ideas; his eyes and ears were wide open. One day, when he stopped in the open-air market to eye the wares at a woman's fruit stand, he asked if I saw the light bulb just go off over his head. The next time he painted a woman he replaced her head with a melon; the next one had a banana for a head. The series was titled *Objectified Women.*

"What the hell?" I said, my nose up against the window, entranced by Verboten's shenanigans. "What's he doing in there?"

"Good question," Vorkuta said.

"We're getting to the bottom of this right now."

"Don't," Vorkuta hissed, pulling at my arm.

But I was moving so fast that my sleeve wrenched out of his grasp. My bad ankle pulled up the rear. I made it in the door of the gallery, where my progress was cut short by a wall that appeared out of nowhere, knocking the air out of my lungs. I dropped to my ass with a thud, clutching my chest. A guy was standing in front of me; his biceps were bigger than my thighs.

"The exhibition hasn't opened yet," said the woman standing next to Verboten. She didn't even glance in my direction.

"Goddammit, Verboten," I groaned.

I tried to get up, but a little pressure to my shoulder was all it took for the wall of meat to keep my butt glued to the butcher paper.

Verboten was holding two of his framed pieces in front of him: *Melon Head* and *Egg Carton Head*.

"Oh, I know her," Verboten said, looking over. "Klaus, you can let her in. Metro, come over here and give us your opinion. What order should we hang these in? In relationship to each other, I mean."

I groaned and stood. Klaus the Wall of Human Meat didn't offer to help me up. I circled around his barrel-like chest; I had to make such a broad arc it felt like I was going around a traffic circle.

"What the hell are you doing here?" I asked, once I made it past Klaus. "And who's the chick?"

"This is Anna Liebe. She runs the gallery. My show is opening here on Friday. And this is Metro, one of my assistants."

"Your assistant?" I cried.

The woman with a lavender bob shook my hand. Her handshake was as cool as her gaze. Her mouth, on the other hand, smiled so broadly that I caught the flicker of a lone gold tooth.

"Yes, Metro has helped me in the execution of some of these works, like the videos. It's impossible to create them without the cooperation of others."

"Oh, isn't that sweet," said Anna Liebe. "We'll have to invite your friend to the opening, then. If she can pull herself away from the other demands on her time, that is."

Liebe emphasized the *if*. It was like the wall Israel was building around the Palestinian areas. If she hadn't said that *if*, I would have told her I couldn't care less and she could keep her shitty art.

"Of course I'll be there," I said.

"I'll mail you an invitation," Liebe said.

"I don't have an address."

We stared each other down until Ms. Purple Bob spun around on her heels and walked into the back room. I wasted no time tearing into Verboten.

"What the hell is all this?"

"I've been working on an exhibition for a long time. This is one of the best-known galleries in Berlin. They want to do a graffiti show. Imagine what an opportunity this is for street art."

"What fucking art? This is nothing but an opportunity for you."

"Actually, all of us benefit from this."

"How?"

"You assisted me. You'll start making a name for yourself."

"I thought I was doing those gigs to pay the rent, so no one would demolish our home."

"You were. For the rent. But the issues are related."

I nodded at the traffic signs. "You didn't do those. They're Smew's."

"The idea was mine."

"Like hell it was!"

"I'm the one who carried the traffic signs into our place. They were there before you guys moved in. Smew just helped with the execution."

"What the hell are you talking about? He's the one who conceived and painted all those."

The sky grew dark overhead. Klaus's shadow fell across me as Anna the gallery owner clacked out of her office in her red heels. She was holding a piece of cardboard. It had a photo of a brick wall glued to it; the text of the invitation had been sprayed across the cardboard surface.

"I hope to see you there," she said in a tone that meant *I hope you go fuck yourself.*

"Every invitation is unique. They're part of a numbered series," Verboten said. "There are only three hundred cards. Make sure you hold on to yours, they're going to rise in value."

"Did you know the Ice Cave has been demolished?" I asked.

"We're in a bit of a rush. We've used all the time we have for this today," Anna Liebe said firmly.

"The whole building was torn down, goddammit! All that's left is a pile of broken bricks and crushed glass."

"I had no idea," Verboten said.

"Weren't you supposed to make sure it stayed standing?"

"Klaus will show you out," Anna said.

I felt viselike pincers clamp down on my shoulders. My shoes started moving across the butcher paper.

"Be sure and come to the opening," Anna said with a toss of her purple bob.

"Smew and Alyosha are dead!" I shouted from under Klaus's elbow. "But I'm sure you know that, since you know fucking everything!"

The mastodon chucked me to the sidewalk. I picked myself up; my jeans had a new hole at the knee. I limped around the corner, now escorted by the cyclopic eye of the surveillance camera. Vorkuta was waiting there in the shadows. He remarked that I had clearly bumped into the same wall of flesh he did when he tried to have a private chat with Verboten.

I peered in through the uncovered strip of window and watched Verboten crouch down and spray through a stencil. Then Klaus's fist appeared at the gap. He pulled the butcher paper all the way to the jamb, and that was it for our peephole.

EASTERN PROMISES

"I thought that man could be you. And we could live here."

I had returned to Dad's place that night. I brought him and Samuel a three-thousand-piece puzzle I lifted from a store. The picture in the puzzle was a marina full of sailboats; in the foreground, there was a mint-green house with an old lady and her cat sitting out front. Lots of open sky. A breakwater stretched out to the edge; a man sat fishing at the tip.

"In some other world, you mean?" Dad frowned.

"In any fucking world."

"Where am I in the picture?" Samuel asked.

"You're out there snorkeling by those rocks with me."

Samuel put together the pieces of sky at a steady, breakneck pace. Dad went and got a magnifying glass from the kitchen drawer and examined the face of the man fishing from the breakwater.

"Well?" I asked, when all he did was sigh.

"This fisherman doesn't look like me," he mumbled.

"You know what I mean," I said with a huff. "When all this is over we'll go on a trip together, somewhere with warm water and sunshine. All three of us."

"I could lose my job over this," Dad said. "And then we won't have money to travel anywhere. I don't even have the money now."

"You're not going to lose anything."

Dad avoided my gaze for a second and then revealed that he had done what I had asked. He'd paid a visit to Himmelkraft Construction Rental. Vorkuta had done something amid the chaos that hadn't occurred to me when we escaped from the Ice Cave. The second we made it down from the collapsing roof he checked the cab of the crane that was swinging the steel ball, looking for some way to identify the company responsible for the demolition. He'd found a name: Himmelkraft. *Force of heaven.*

That was the difference between Vorkuta and me. His head worked even when he was panicking.

While Vorkuta searched for Verboten in the days following the destruction of the Ice Cave, he also located the Himmelkraft headquarters in Marzahn, on the eastern edge of Berlin. During the Berlin Olympics of 1936, Marzahn had been the site of a concentration camp where Roma and other overly dusky people such as myself had been dragged to make sure they didn't offend the eyes of Olympic visitors. Now an enormous ten-hectare industrial park was being built in the same spot, and Himmelkraft was participating by leasing construction equipment to the building sites sprouting up around it.

At my request, or actually demand, Dad had put on his security guard uniform and paid a visit to the portable trailer that served as Himmelkraft HQ. He told them he was there about a building that had just been demolished near the Jewish cemetery at Weissensee. A map was consulted.

Dad lied to the person at the office, explaining that there was an empty five-story warehouse next to the demolished building and he was the guard who worked there. The owner of the warehouse was interested in using Himmelkraft to tear down his building. But before the owner made his final decision, he wanted to hear what the company that had hired Himmelkraft said about the quality of Himmelkraft's demolition services. Dad had been sent to ask for the contact information of the company that had hired Himmelkraft.

The folks at the Himmelkraft offices wondered why a matter like this wasn't handled by e-mail or phone. *Old people, old-fashioned ways,* Dad said with an irritated snort. *There are owners, and then there are servants who run around doing the owners' bidding, relying on their own two feet, not phone lines or cell phone towers. Skin color has nothing to do with it. Or so they insist. The owner's dogs get better food than I do.* This had elicited a smile from the clerk; she had delved into her files and placed in Dad's hand the name and address of the company that had been invoiced for demolition of the Ice Cave.

The name of the company was Eastern Promises.

"Eastern Promises is owned by someone named Pavel Putikov," Dad said, handing me the page torn out of his notebook where he had jotted down Putikov's name and that of his company. "That's all I know. And there's no way I'm going to go ask more questions. You have to forget the whole thing, Maria."

"Yeah, yeah," I said. On the next page of the notebook, I drew Samuel's name in puzzle style. I occasionally used puzzle style when spraying my name on a wall. The letters are formed with puzzle pieces, so it takes time; you can't use puzzle style if you're afraid some guard is breathing down your neck. I added shadows and handed the paper to Samuel.

"Whoaaaaa," he shrieked, clenching it to his chest.

The gesture warmed my heart more than any words could have. He wanted me to hang the piece of paper on the wall over his bed.

After Dad and Samuel fell asleep, I started up the recording. I wanted to see who entered and exited the Ice Cave after Smew and

Alyosha were dropped from the beam. Who had arranged for Banksy's piece to be hoisted out through the roof right after the murders? Who scrubbed the Ice Cave into the spiffy condition it was in when I showed up a couple of days later, after my recovery at American Buffalo's?

It was impossible to tell from the footage. The recording ended with Smew and Alyosha being dropped.

The beginning of the recording had weeks' worth of images of the five of us entering and exiting. Slipping into the Ice Cave and back out again, walking along the beam in our different styles. But Smew never changed the memory card, and, of course, it cut off at the very second when something out of the ordinary and worth recording happened.

Shitty luck.

After I'd watched through the final minutes of the recording over and over again, I was sure about one thing, though. Smew was still alive when they rolled him down from the beam. His hand rose and his fingers grasped empty air as he fell.

He tried to grab at nothing as if it were a lifeline.

PEST CONTROL

While I was playing house and doing puzzles with Samuel, Vorkuta lurked outside the gallery, waiting for a moment when Verboten would leave alone. The first night was a bust; Verboten never emerged. Vorkuta dropped by the following morning to let me know that even summer nights can be damn cold if you spend them out in the open air.

During his next stakeout, Vorkuta slipped into the backyard for a piss and discovered the gallery had a back door. He started watching it. Sure enough, Verboten left the gallery around seven that evening. Vorkuta stayed on the opposite side of the street and shadowed him for about a kilometer to a three-star hotel. Through the glass door, he saw Verboten ask at the reception desk for his key, the kind with a half-kilo club attached to it so you can't forget it in your pocket when you leave the hotel. Vorkuta stepped into the lobby. The eagle-eyed clerk shot out from behind the counter to inquire as to the nature of his business, and Vorkuta retreated.

On the third night, Vorkuta hung out in front of the gallery; I waited in the junk-filled courtyard out back. I was sharing it with a scruffy, one-eyed cat, and she gave me an evil look, as if I had invaded her kingdom. She had a litter of tiny, still-blind kittens in a small nook she guarded, hissing.

I was silently hissing to myself, too. Verboten reminded me of Baron, an ex-friend of mine from Finland. I had trusted him when some security guards were hunting me down, but he'd told them where I was hiding to save his own skin and his future and his company car, an Audi with a smiling house on the side.

At eight thirty, the back door opened and Verboten stepped out. I was waiting behind the Dumpsters with the claw-baring, one-eyed wildcat.

I had borrowed a cell phone from my dad, and I placed a silent call to Vorkuta. I didn't want him to answer; I just wanted him to know that Verboten had exited the building by the rear door. He caught up to me at the next corner and immediately raced ahead to circle around.

Verboten headed for his hotel at a brisk pace. I had a hard time keeping up, even though I had learned to swing myself forward on my lone crutch more quickly than most people managed on two legs. I caught up to him at a cigarette machine.

"How's it going?" I said.

"Metro," he sputtered.

"A moment of your time. Nonnegotiable."

"I can't, sorry. The exhibition opens tomorrow, and there's still a hell of a lot to do."

Verboten strode off, putting some space between me and him, and stepped into traffic. He ignored the blaring horns.

So did I.

The cars were more willing to cede territory to a woman on crutches than to Verboten. He marched purposefully up the sidewalk, dodging oncoming pedestrians. I did my best to stay on his heels, but the crutch made it tough to weave through the crowd, and I kept banging into people.

Verboten was getting well ahead of me and would have gotten away if it weren't for Vorkuta, who had circled around in front of us. When Verboten was looking back at me, Vorkuta tackled him from his blind side, pushing him in through a pub door concealed in an awning's shadow.

By the time I entered the pub, Vorkuta had dragged Verboten over to the corner booth. I took a seat across from Verboten and blocked his exit route with a crosswise crutch. Vorkuta went and ordered us beers. They were warm; the bar's refrigeration system was busted. Vorkuta took a seat next to Verboten, crushing him against the side of the booth. There was no way Verboten could get out without climbing over Vorkuta.

"*Prosit*," I said.

"No, thanks. I don't drink beer," Verboten replied.

"This isn't beer, this is piss," I said. "Perfect for dickheads."

Vorkuta had selected the dive bar as a place to confront Verboten since his hotel was under the strictest surveillance. Apparently the pub had been nearly empty the day before when Vorkuta had dropped in. A few guys had been slouching around the back table, their hands petrified around the handles of their pints. According to Vorkuta, the bunch slumped back there tonight was the same crew. The pallor on their faces reminded me of wax dolls.

"You killed Smew and Alyosha," I said.

"No, I didn't," Verboten snapped. "You two are totally fucking delusional."

He didn't say much else for a minute, because Vorkuta elbowed him in the diaphragm under the table. Verboten gasped for air like a beached flounder.

"I have a recording that proves you were in the Ice Cave when Smew and Alyosha were murdered," I said as he wheezed. I explained what I had seen him do in the video, how he led the killers in, and what had taken place in the Ice Cave afterward. I told him what I had seen with my own two eyes when I showed up at the Ice Cave that morning after getting my X-rays, the puddles of blood and the bodies, and how I had run and hidden from the killers. I told him what Vorkuta had witnessed earlier, and how the Banksy piece, or actually the entire wall, had been lifted out through a hole in the metal roof.

"That's how delusional we are," I finished.

"They weren't supposed to do anything to Smew and Alyosha," Verboten mumbled. "You guys have to believe me. I wasn't there anymore when they killed them. I was just supposed to show them where *Ice Rat* was. Then I was free to go. They said that all they wanted was Banksy's work. They'd gently hoist the wall out with a crane."

"They, who?"

"The people sponsoring my show at the gallery."

"What the hell?" I shouted.

Vorkuta gave me a cautioning look and nodded toward the table in back. None of the wax dolls appeared to react in the slightest to my outburst. Behind the counter, the bartender was riveted by the soccer match playing on his tiny television screen. A cigarette smoldered in his lips. A NO SMOKING sign hung above the bar.

"Do you seriously think I was planning on staying in the Ice Cave forever?" Verboten asked. "That building had a death sentence hanging over it long before you guys showed up. You should be grateful you got to live there as long as you did."

Verboten would have said more but Vorkuta elbowed him in the gut again. We had to wait for Verboten to catch his breath. One of the regulars in back started pounding his empty pint glass against the tabletop and squawking loudly in irritation. He calmed down when the bartender carried over a fresh pint and removed the one that had been drained dry.

"This is all about Pest Control," Verboten gasped.

Now it was Vorkuta's turn to shout. "Pest control? So we were pests, huh? And Alyosha was a real special kind of pest?" He gave Verboten some more elbow.

When Verboten was capable of talking between wheezes again I learned about Banksy's Pest Control. When Banksy had bunked at the Ice Cave years ago he wasn't a global star. No one knew him except his buddies from Bristol. No one wanted his work. Verboten had shown him around town and pointed out good places to paint. All the other Banksy pieces eventually disappeared; the attic wall was the only one left. The only ones who knew about its existence were Banksy and Verboten. And Pest Control.

When Banksy rose to fame the market for his work became insane. His pieces were removed from walls; a lot of forgeries appeared, too.

During the early stages of his career, Banksy sold works he painted on paper for a few dozen pounds; suddenly those same pieces were bringing in thousands. They were cash cows making the rounds from intermediary to intermediary.

Banksy hit the brakes and founded Pest Control, which certified his work as genuine. Or didn't. Before long, Pest Control had absolute control over the Banksy resale market: its word determined if a Banksy being sold was genuine. But authenticity didn't depend on whether or not Banksy had done the work, but on whether or not it had a certificate of authenticity. A certificate of authenticity was granted for a print belonging to one of Banksy's numbered series if the buyer had acquired the work from one of the intermediaries Banksy trusted. There was nothing Banksy hated more than the resale of works he had already sold once, and for that reason Pest Control was very stingy about granting certificates of authenticity to galleries that were known to accumulate Banksys in an attempt to sell them at a profit.

Certificates of authenticity were also granted for paintings Banksy had created for his own exhibitions. Sometimes Banksy refused to sell to people whose personal values didn't jibe with his.

Pest Control's strict policy meant that the prices of Banksy works with a certificate of authenticity were stratospheric, especially if the works were unique and not part of a numbered series. The value of an uncertified Banksy was zilch. Some of Banksy's old friends who'd wanted to cash in on an early Banksy they'd received for free could bitterly attest to this.

Pest Control was the Supreme Court of the graffiti world. There was no appealing its decisions.

In some perverse, absurd way, this way of doing things suited the ideology of a man who dissed art created for art's sake.

The Pest Control system treated Banksy's bigger street pieces as a class of their own. Pest Control unequivocally and categorically refused to grant certificates of authenticity to any of Banksy's public murals. In Banksy's view, they were intended for everyone, not for galleries or museums or private collections, and especially not as commodities for wheeling and dealing.

Ice Rat was the sole exception.

Right after it was founded, Pest Control sent a certificate of authenticity for *Ice Rat* to Verboten's PO box. It was accompanied by the requisite half of a ten-pound Banksy note, adorned with Princess Diana instead of Queen Elizabeth. The same series number appeared on both halves of the bill; Pest Control held on to the other half. The series number for *Ice Rat* was BY00000001—it was the first piece certified as a genuine Banksy by Pest Control.

Banksy wanted to grant *Ice Rat* a certificate of authenticity because the idea for Pest Control certificates had been inspired by a motif that appeared in the piece: a bill that had been sliced in half by an ice skate.

Verboten agreed to let *Ice Rat* live out its natural life-span. He would allow it to be destroyed when the building was eventually demolished. Verboten also promised not to reveal *Ice Rat*'s existence to anyone except the select few who stayed in the Ice Cave. No one would ever find out who was behind the piece.

"Banksy's work isn't any better than the stuff other writers do," Verboten spat between clenched teeth. This was the guy who had sworn to seal his lips forever about the certificate of authenticity granted to *Ice Rat*. "The guy's a mediocre copycat at best. He bit the rat motif from that French guy, Blek le Rat. He's sold himself to the business world and now he wants to stop other people from getting rich the same way. Banksy lives like the British aristocracy back in the day. For all he cares the rest of us can be penniless paupers, as long as his country house is freshly painted, and champagne flows from the fountains onto mani-cured lawns, and the servants are running around polishing the silver and emptying the piss pots. If Banksy were a real fucking writer he'd share the wealth he's accumulated with other graffiti artists! If he were a real communist."

"Communist?" Vorkuta barked. "Do you even know any communists?"

"I'm a communist," Verboten said with an injured air. "You guys got to live in my commune, basically for free."

"You're exactly the same as the communists back home."

"Thanks. That's a real compliment, coming from a Russian."

"The only thing Soviet commies were interested in was personal gain, not shared prosperity. Just like you," Vorkuta said, spitting in Verboten's pint. "I hate bullshit ideologies so much."

"What is it you guys want?" Verboten asked, staring at the surface of his beer. "I can get you a chance to have your own show. Anna has good contacts in the art world."

"You can shove the art world up your artsy ass," I said.

"Metro, you've always been so hostile," Verboten said, shaking his head. "You're carrying around a bucket of coal-black hatred inside you. I never should have let you stay at the Ice Cave. You've been nothing but trouble."

"So I'm the one who killed Smew?"

"There's no problem that can't be solved by negotiation," Verboten said. "There's no need for violence. Try turning your bucket of hatred upside down. You might find a drop of positivity at the bottom. A healthy entrepreneurial spirit."

"What planet are you living on?" I hissed. "Thanks to your greed Smew and Alyosha are dead."

"An unfortunate accident. I wasn't aware of the complications."

"Why don't we forget these complications of yours," Vorkuta said. "There's only one thing we want. We want to know where *Ice Rat* is and who took it."

"That's two things," Verboten said, raising a forefinger and a middle finger.

It was all he had time for. Vorkuta bashed his face into the table. Verboten cried out that he didn't know, but that Anna Liebe had connections. She could make discreet inquiries and give us the information at the exhibition opening. We headed out and left Verboten slumped next to his beer.

"That's what happens when you don't offer your pals a pint," one of the drunks at the round table loudly explained to his companions, indicating Verboten, who was trying to stanch the blood flowing from his nose. "Now someone better buy another round."

THE OBSCURE OBJECT OF HIS LUST

By the time Vorkuta and I showed up at the opening, the gallery was teeming with guests. A tight ring had formed around Verboten; the only parts of him you could see were the nonstop smile and his hand clinking champagne flutes with the latest congratulators. A waiter in black held out a tray toward us, too, but the thing that lifted my spirits more than the glass of bubbly was Verboten's swollen nose and his scarred face, which today was ruddier than usual.

As we waited for a gap to open up in the ring, we emptied the buffet table. Klaus and his broad shoulders had been commandeered to pour punch and greet guests. He had also been taught to smile for the event; I heard his teeth grind as he politely wished me a good evening. A chubby guy in a suit across the punch bowl from me was wearing a tie embellished with a stick figure drawn by his three-year-old. I guess he figured it would help him blend into the graffiti tribe.

A continuous stream of well-wishers was gathering in a vaulted alcove off the gallery. I forced my way through the crowd to have a look at what everyone was gawking at. What I found was video footage of a glass high-rise I knew all too well, one facade covered with a giant car ad. Concrete barriers with metal bars protruding from them had been brought in and arranged on the floor in front of the video wall. Sturdy orange plastic mesh was lashed between the bars, the same kind of mesh found in the stairwell outside the Ice Cave and downstairs to keep people from climbing up to the higher floors without permission.

The barrier read VERBOTEN, followed by a shitload of exclamation points.

Apparently Verboten had snagged some plastic netting from the building before it was torn down. Or asked the demolition crew to bring him a selection.

A flashing light had been installed on the ceiling next to the video to create the impression of an approaching police car. The sirens were nearly drowned out by the babel of the guests.

I watched Alyosha and me descend the high-rise on unsteady ropes, writing across the ad as we dropped. The crowd clapped when we leapt the final meters to the asphalt and Alyosha half carried, half led me away. The sirens on the recording grew louder and louder. The video ended with an image of police officers clustered below the empty, swinging ropes and the bombed billboard.

The title of the work—*Baby Killers! Gun Runners! Genocidal Maniacs!*—had been taken from the text Alyosha and I had painted. Verboten had been noted as the artist, and the price had been set at thirty thousand euros. The work was already marked SOLD.

Other videos were playing elsewhere in the space, including the video of our train job, which I had already seen. All the painting we had done "for the common good" had ended up for sale, with Verboten's name underneath. There was no mention of Smew as the videographer.

A coffin with Verboten's signature on the side occupied one corner of the gallery. A video clip projected on the wall behind it showed Verboten rising from his trunk in the Ice Cave, the candelabra glowing, a black cape at his shoulders, a grim look in his eyes as he stared at the camera. He was holding a can of spray paint, and he threw up a message on the attic wall: FUCK THE VAMPIRES. VERBOTEN—THE TRUE RULER OF THE NIGHT. I remembered when Smew had filmed this as a joke. But from my current vantage point, screwing with Verboten didn't strike me as funny at all.

I took a look at the ceiling. A swarm of at least twenty surveillance cameras had been installed in one corner, where they droned in agitated circles. That little piece also had a title and a price.

A blank space had been left along one wall, next to Verboten's big-breasted female figures. It was the guest book; we all were expected to spray our signatures in it. The roly-poly guy with the stick-figure tie was just spraying a stick figure next to his name. The tie hadn't been his kid's handiwork, after all; it was all him. The crowd clapped wildly for Chubbykins.

I stretched my neck to see what Verboten had titled the women he had painted, the ones with an iron or a television or a watermelon or a banana for a head: *Verboten Venus of Willendorf I*, *Verboten Venus of Willendorf II*, *Verboten Venus of Willendorf III*, and so on, all the way up to fifteen.

Now I knew what it felt like to die and go to hell.

Vorkuta had gotten stuck watching Alyosha's descent from the glass high-rise over and over. I fetched another drink and put it in his hand.

When I waved at Verboten to catch his attention, the gallery harpy, Anna Liebe, caught sight of me. She tried to eviscerate me with a look; her fake eyelashes flashed like sabers. She started heading over, but on her way she spotted a bald guy in black who had just walked in. She executed a quick change of direction, swooped over to catch Verboten, and dragged him over to shake hands with the skinhead.

"Simply superb," said a woman in polka dots who had appeared at my side. "Such intensity," she said with a sigh. "It's almost as if they're talking."

I finally realized she was directing this drivel at me; at first I thought she was just talking to herself.

"Who's talking?" I asked. "Those surveillance cameras?"

"No, no, those traffic signs. They refuse to be satisfied with seeing. They demand the right to speak."

"They're metal."

"They're voices, speaking out on behalf of free speech."

"You can have it for a price," I said. "Your own bit of free speech."

"Yes." She nodded enthusiastically. "A brilliant investment. They're definitely going to go up in price. Clearly undervaluated."

"How much are they?"

"Five each."

"Five what? Bananas?"

"Thousand."

"What the fuck?" I blurted out.

"I know, I know. Such a bargain."

Solemnly, she stepped over to study one of the road signs Smew had painted. Back in the Ice Cave, Smew had added nipples to the black mounds on either side of the UNEVEN ROAD, and between the breasts thus formed he had painted a man in a tie ogling them. Verboten had signed the traffic sign as his own and called it *The Obscure Object of His Lust*.

I made my way over to Vorkuta.

"I'm gonna barf pretty soon," I said.

Vorkuta nodded in agreement. We went and hovered like hawks, waiting for the moment Verboten would end his chat with baldy. When he did I snatched his sleeve and pointed forcefully at the alcove where I was descending through the sky over and over again, the shemagh covering my face.

"Sorry. Big buyer," Verboten explained.

"Who? That bald undertaker?"

"He's American. Owns several galleries and promised to arrange a show for me in Los Angeles. Apparently Hollywood is crazy about street art."

Verboten pulled back a curtain and steered me through a door behind it into a long room where shipping crates were stacked along the walls. A basket on the table was overflowing with cans of spray paint and caps. Next to them was a big calculator; it was the perfect instrument for Verboten's kind of writing. Vorkuta stayed outside, leaning against the door, to act as lookout.

"It's better for us to talk back here," Verboten said. "Those surveillance cameras out in the gallery work."

"Why?"

"I'm going to turn the footage into a piece of art."

"You suck, man. Is there a single principle of yours you haven't totally raped yet?"

Verboten didn't even raise an eyebrow. He reached into his pocket and handed me a folded piece of paper. I glanced at it. A familiar name was scrawled on it: Pavel Putikov. But the address was even more familiar.

"What the fuck are you trying to pull? This place is in Finland. Near my hometown."

"Putikov has a summer place there. That's where the Banksy piece is going to end up. Putikov has built an amazing space for his art collection at his dacha."

"You're lying. Vorkuta read online that *Ice Rat* is going to be auctioned here in Berlin. It's been listed by Grisebach, starting price half a million euros."

Verboten tilted his head. I used to think that I knew what this meant, but not anymore.

"The auction is a smoke screen," he said. "They just want the world at large to know that *Ice Rat* exists. That and the fact that it's the only one of Banksy's murals with a Pest Control certificate of authenticity.

Once that's been established and a price has been publicly determined, that's going to add value to Putikov's collection."

"You're lying," I repeated, less certain of myself.

"In the end, an anonymous investor will bid for it over the phone. The more he bids, the higher the work's value will rise in the eyes of the art world. But Putikov isn't going to pay the auction house a single cent for *Ice Rat*. It's already his. It's a publicity stunt, pure and simple."

Loud voices could be heard coming from outside. The door banged a couple of times, as if Vorkuta were being shoved against it.

"You don't want to end up in these people's crosshairs," Verboten said quickly. "Smew and Alyosha had really shitty luck. It's sad, really sad. But what happened to them isn't our fault. It's not yours and it's not mine. The second Alyosha came back from the emergency room where he left you I told them to clear out of the Ice Cave. They did, but they snuck back in without me knowing it. I told them to stay away that whole night. I made it very clear."

"How can you even sleep at night?"

"Believe me, Metro," Verboten said. "I didn't want any harm to come to anyone."

"I don't believe a word you say about anything anymore."

Before I could finish my sentence, Verboten grabbed me in his arms and kissed me on the lips. I was so flabbergasted I didn't have the sense to bite off the tongue that slithered into my mouth. Behind us, the door crashed open and a gasp of surprise darted our way from the threshold. Verboten squeezed me a moment longer before pulling back.

"We thought something was wrong in here," Anna Liebe said from the doorway. "Apologies for the disturbance," she added coolly, eyeing first me and then Verboten.

"We're fine. Metro just missed me," Verboten said, winking at Anna. "She was incredibly depressed for a long time after I broke up with her. Came here to beg me to get back together with her. I said no, but she attacked me. I didn't do anything to encourage her. We can't help how attractive other people find us, can we?"

"You go fuck—" I started, before noticing Klaus standing behind Anna. He had Vorkuta's head trapped under his arm. Vorkuta's face was crimson.

"Hot kisses, hot memories, but we have to face the facts, my little Metro," Verboten said. "We're not meant for each other. This was the last time. Next time I'll be forced to press sexual harassment charges."

Verboten grabbed me by the elbow, steered me past Anna and out of the back room; he wished me a nice life and wandered off to converse with some art journalist, champagne flute in hand. A second later, a dozen other people were milling around him.

Vorkuta appeared at my side, all bent out of shape.

"Let's go," I said.

"That guy tried to crush me," Vorkuta croaked. "He cracked the fucking vertebrae in my neck."

I glanced at the roving cameras spying from the ceiling and propelled Vorkuta against the current toward the front door and the darkened city outside.

"I didn't know you and Verboten had a thing."

"I didn't, either."

When we had finally put a couple of blocks between us and the gallery I showed Vorkuta the paper Verboten had slipped me and repeated the background story.

Once we'd walked a bit more it was clear we were being followed.

We climbed Warschauer Strasse; the tracks and zooming trains flashed past below. I took a sudden right up to a Z-shaped overpass leading across the tracks toward Warschauer Strasse Station. The two men I had noticed at the bottom of the hill turned to follow us. From my elevated vantage point I could see a train from the city center approaching the station from the north.

I rushed Vorkuta down the stairs. When the men saw us making for the approaching train they started running across the overpass. It wouldn't be long before they were within a few dozen meters of us.

A freight train was approaching from the south; it would pass along the track closest to the platform.

The slip of paper Verboten had given me was burning a hole in my pocket.

The S-Bahn stopped and opened its doors; passengers spilled out onto the platform. The two men had made it down the stairs. They were both Klaus's size and looked equally unfriendly.

The headlights of the approaching freight train blazed like the eyes of a lion.

"You're going to have to help me," I said to Vorkuta.

There was no response. Vorkuta never asked pointless questions. He wrapped his arm around me and leapt; I pushed off as best I could with my good leg. We flew across the track, barely missing the nose of the freight train.

NAKED ON AN ANTHILL

The brakes squealed as the freight train passing Warschauer Strasse Station came to a stop; a shrill shriek rose above the squeal. A woman thought we'd been hit by the train.

Vorkuta dragged me to my feet on the far side of the tracks. My crutch had flown out of my hand during our leap. I limped over, snatched it up, and climbed up the strip of land behind the track.

Behind us, the train was still braking. The two locomotives were pulling tank cars; the tracks were spitting out sparks. A barricade of dozens of tank cars was blocking the path between our pursuers and us.

We crossed the embankment and threw ourselves over the chain-link fence, tumbling into a rail yard. Empty tracks were followed by a freight train parked crosswise in front of us. It was all boxcars—a graffiti artist's mobile art gallery, its walls just waiting to be painted. But there was no time for that now.

We crossed the tracks and Vorkuta helped me clamber between two of the boxcars. He climbed up the ladder at the end of one of the cars, scanning the terrain like a sailor peering out from the crow's nest of an old sailing ship.

The engineer behind us had finally managed to get his tanker train to stop.

"They're following us," Vorkuta said. "They're coming between the tank cars."

"How many?"

"Two."

"They don't necessarily mean us any harm."

"Yeah, right," Vorkuta said drily.

A passenger train whooshed past on the next track; the lights reflecting from its windows cast leopard-like spots on the ground.

"There's no way we're going to make it across the tracks to those warehouses," Vorkuta said, assessing the route between the freight trains. "At least *you* won't with that leg."

There were six tracks between us and the warehouses at the edge of Warschauer Strasse Station. The rail yard was well lit and there was no cover. We may as well have tried to ride tricycles down a runway in broad daylight and hoped no one in the air traffic control tower noticed.

But rail yards were my terrain. I knew how to find the best hiding spots.

"Under the bridge," I said.

In Kotka, the night Rust died, security guards had been spying on us from the shadows of a bridge. We hadn't noticed them, even though our antennae had been tuned in to possible threats.

Under cover of the boxcars, Vorkuta and I made for Warschauer Strasse Bridge, which ran across the tracks. He peered under the train to the other side.

"We're not even going to make it to the overpass," he whispered. "They're fast. They're already at the fence."

We made it to the final boxcar and hid behind it. It was about forty more meters to the first pillar supporting the overpass.

"Don't do it, Metro," Vorkuta said when he saw me eyeing the distance.

He crouched down and watched our pursuers step into the well-lit rail yard from between two boxcars.

At first they scanned the flat area spreading out before them. Yet another train sped past. I saw the windows of a restaurant car and caught some woman in it holding up her fork in a sign of victory.

One of the men climbed up on top of the train, checking to make sure we weren't lying flat on the roof of a boxcar. As soon as he came back down, the men split up. They started heading down either side of the freight train in opposite directions, systematically checking between the cars to make sure they got both sides of the train. The only hiding place was at the butt end of the last car, where we were waiting and watching them.

The men tried the boxcars' sliding doors. They were all locked. One of them headed in our direction; something gleamed in his hand.

"Fuck," I hissed.

"Follow me," Vorkuta whispered in my ear. "Stay low so we don't reflect any light."

He immediately started climbing the ladder at the end of the boxcar and disappeared onto the roof. I followed him up and lay as flat as possible, with my face toward the ladder. Vorkuta had advanced to the other end of the car.

We waited.

Gravel crunched behind me and to the side. Silence, then a clunk. Our pursuer was trying to open the sliding door of the next-to-last boxcar. More crunching gravel. The footfalls died when he got to where Vorkuta was.

I had an urge to run as fast as I could. Straight ahead, despite the fact that I was lying on the roof of a train, despite the fact that one of my legs was half-crippled. But hey, you can run through the air if you just move your limbs fast enough, right?

More crunches. Our pursuer was advancing alongside our car. He tried the sliding door. Then he reached the end of the train.

It was as silent as the grave down below. He must have been eyeing the vicinity to see if he could spot anything out of the ordinary. The rumble of traffic from Warschauer Strasse mingled with the rush of blood in my ears.

I dug my fingers into my thighs so they wouldn't nervously tap the roof of the car. I was sweating and freezing at the same time.

I heard him start climbing the ladder.

Silence again. For some reason, he had stopped halfway up.

My throat tickled. I felt like shouting. I felt like running. I shifted my hand to my crutch.

A faint click. The climbing continued. The fingers of a left hand appeared at the edge of the roof.

I held my breath.

A right hand appeared, too. It was holding a pistol.

The instant the head rose over the edge of the roof, I slammed my crutch into it as hard as I could.

I heard a gasp, the head fell backward, and then both hands disappeared. There was a thud below.

I crawled to the ladder and peered down. The guy was on his back across the tracks; the gun was still in his hand. I scrambled down the ladder, dropped to the gravel, grabbed the pistol, and limped to the overpass, where I hid in the shadows of the pillars. I made sure to keep the rear of the train between me and the guy checking out the front of the train.

Vorkuta scrambled over to my side.

We pressed ourselves against the pillars. I moved on to the next pillar under the cover of a slanted shadow. I could make out a dark figure at the front of the train. He still had to check a few boxcars and the locomotives.

Following the shadows cast by the pillars we made our way to the warehouses; once we got there, I dropped the gun into a Dumpster that reeked of rotten food. Big pieces had been painted on the ends of the buildings. Vorkuta lifted up the chain-link fence so I'd be able to crawl under it into some bushes and through the bushes to the street.

I looked back one final time. A woman was painted on the nearest building. She was naked except for the contour lines they use on maps; they gave shape to her unclothed body, revealing its curves and mounds. Her open mouth screamed as huge red and black ants climbed up her arms and legs.

That's exactly how I felt. Like I was sitting on an anthill, totally naked.

SHOE FLY

Hey, Baron Fuckface!

What's new? Have your sins driven you to suicide yet? If not, I want you to look into this one house for me. And this time you'd better not say a peep to anyone about what you're doing, goddammit. If you don't do what I ask you to or I suspect you of squealing, I'm going to upload 10,000 naked pictures of little kids to your computer and tip off the police and the National Bureau of Investigation that there's a pedophile using his real estate business to expand his kiddie porn ring. All I have to do is press Enter once and you're done.

A buddy and I are coming up there to the butthole of the world; he's never seen a man who wears a suit year in, year out. See, you're as rare as a bamboo-munching panda. I told him that you're under doctor's orders to dress up; if you're not allowed to wrap a tie around your neck every day, you'll tighten a noose around your neck.

A pair of small, cool palms lowering in front of my eyes interrupted me.

"Let's go," Samuel said.

"I told you, I'll be right there. Dad's going to take you to the park
first, and I'm going to follow you guys."

"No, come now."

"I have to finish writing this."

"What does it say? Read it to me!"

"It's pretty hard to read when I can't see anything."

The tiny fingers covering my left eye spread a little.

"It reads that Samuel has to go to the park now."

"No, it doesn't," Samuel said, jabbing a fingertip at the screen. "I
can read it."

"You don't know how to read, sorry."

"Do, too. Blahblahblah poopoopeepeepoopoo. Blahblahblahblah.
Fuckfuckfuckfuck. Susususususususuuu."

"Yup, that's exactly what it says. Now let me finish this."

"Maria, are you teaching Samuel swear words?"

"No."

The palms fell from my eyes and Samuel disappeared somewhere
behind me. Dad was clattering in the kitchen. Samuel went to take over.
He was better at fixing leaking faucets than Dad was. Then he showed
him how I'd taught him that if something didn't work all you had to do
was kick it and shout *shit fuck motherfucker*. They're the magic words.

> I'll be in touch when I get there; I expect
> you to have all the information by then. God
> help me, you'd better work on selling those
> moldy apartments of yours some other day.
> This is your one and only chance to try and
> make up for even a hundredth of the bullshit
> you pulled, you goddamn rat. Smew says

hi, he's having the time of his life. His work
has been shown in a big exhibition here, and
people have been admiring it as far away as
the United States. He's been shooting video,
too. I wouldn't be surprised if he became a
movie director in Hollywood someday.

The racket behind me grew louder. Dad was trying to tie Samuel's shoelaces, but Samuel kept pulling his foot away.

"I'm not going till Metro comes."

"Her name is Maria."

"I don't want to go!"

"Samuel, I'll come as soon as I finish this," I said, raising three fingers. "Scout's honor."

"I'm not going," Samuel said. He collapsed to the floor, arms and legs spread, like he was making a snow angel. He must have quadrupled his weight by force of thought, because Dad couldn't lift him, even though he strained until he was red in the face.

"Wait a sec," I said. I went and got my leather jacket from the coatrack and handed it to Dad. "Take my coat to the park with you. Samuel, it's your job to make sure nothing happens to it."

"What on earth am I going to do with your coat?"

"Keep your eyes peeled," I stressed to Samuel. "Show that ugly guard how badass coat ninjas are."

"Coat ninjas?" Samuel asked.

"Don't let that coat out of your sight. Follow it wherever it goes. Spy on it without him knowing. A real coat ninja knows where the nearest security guard in a leather coat is creeping around, even in his sleep."

"Ha-ha," Dad said.

"Ha-ha to you, too. Some people are plain old security guards. Other people are coat ninjas."

I've met my little brother and spent the last
few days staying at Dad's place. For years I
thought he was a total prick, but he's cooler
than I thought. We've been doing puzzles
together. My five-year-old brother can do
them a hundred times faster than I can. I'm
going to teach him to become the best graffiti artist ever; we've already practiced in a
couple of courtyards. His name is Samuel.
Once he learns the alphabet he'll be the best
writer ever. He's still a little heavy on the
freestyle. I've been thinking I could maybe
live here with Dad for a while; we didn't see
each other for so many years. I've had more
than enough of Mom and her BS up in Kotka.
Samuel is the coolest kid I've ever met.
Normally, kids stink and bawl and bump into
walls and barf when they're high on sugar,
and the rest of the time they're sick.

I glanced out the window. Dad was just exiting the building with
Samuel. He was wearing my leather jacket. It was only now that I realized how much Dad and I looked alike. We were about the same height,
we had the same kind of chronically messy hair, and over the past few
days Dad's halfhearted stride had reclaimed some of its former feline
lightness, like mine.

It was almost like I was watching myself from above.

Samuel hid behind a lamppost to spy on Dad. Dad was forced to
walk over and take him by the hand to get him to the crosswalk, where
they waited for the light to change.

Samuel turned toward the window. I waved. I pointed my forefinger and middle finger at my eyes and then at the back of Dad's leather coat. *Stay on him. Don't let him out of your sight.*

Samuel nodded, and the light turned green. He bounded a couple of meters behind the leather jacket like a little panther on the prowl. Halfway across the crosswalk he turned back to the window.

I showed him my fingers again. *Stay on him. Follow the target.*

I caught a dark streak out of the corner of my eye.

The next instant, a black car crashed into Dad full force and raced toward the next corner at incredible speed.

Samuel stood there in the middle of the road.

Dad had been thrown several meters. He was motionless on the ground. His shoe had flown into the air; it spun there in the sky for what seemed like an eternity.

A puddle immediately started spreading out around Dad's head. My leather jacket covered his back, which had snapped in the middle like a broken branch. He was dead.

I was the one lying there on the asphalt. Or I should have been. Not Dad.

The world was stone. Dad had turned to stone. Samuel was stone. I was stone. Not a single passerby moved. The only moving thing in this stone world was a black car that had sped off and vanished blocks away. And a shoe that finally rolled into the street after tumbling across the asphalt countless times.

III: THE RAT IN THE CASTLE

PARADISE

The place looked like a castle that had been carted over from Scotland, a fortress built to defend residents against invitations to haggis parties, as well as the occasional intruder. It had a crenellated tower made from massive blocks of red and gray granite; instead of the usual guards, a satellite dish stood watch at the top. The foundation, which was well over a meter tall, was made of hunks of the same granite, with letters and symbols engraved in them.

Baron whispered in my ear that the owner had wanted them to look like blocks of stone quarried by Italian Renaissance stonemasons; the stoneworkers of the past hammered their initials into every block they cut.

"These rocks were quarried by machine," Baron said. "But the initials make it look like handiwork. You probably noticed the extremely rare orbicular granite appearing primarily near the main door. It's only found in a couple of locations in Finland. That's from Virvik, in Porvoo."

Above its reddish stone foundation the manor house was finished in mint-green stucco.

"How many centuries old is it?" I asked.

"It's been under construction for less than a year. There's a big basement, including a wine cellar."

"How do you know?"

"I visited once, as a guest, in the role of real estate agent."

Baron was spying on the manor grounds through his binoculars. After having not seen him in over six months it was hard to get used to the fact that he spoke so formally. We were lying in tall grass, in the shadow of some birches. The mosquitos whined tirelessly in our ears.

"I only see two surveillance cameras," he said.

"That's weird."

"Not necessarily. The owner has such a formidable reputation that no one dares drop by unannounced."

"You mean Putikov?"

In addition to the stone tower with the parapet, the manor had a lower, squatter tower finished in wood. I could make out a table and sun chairs on top of it. Instead of a whole fence, the castle had only a wrought-iron gate out front, with a two-headed eagle worked into it. The spikes stabbing up from the gate glowed like golden spear tips.

"Couldn't he afford the whole fence?" I asked.

"That gate is from the tsar's summer palace. Janus doesn't need a fence to protect him. The gate is one of the works from his collection."

"Janus?"

The mint-green manor only had two stories, but the rooms were so tall that one of the four-story apartment buildings from the concrete ghetto I grew up in would have been no bigger, even with the twenty families that lived in it. The main entrance was a double door as tall as the wrought-iron gate, bordered by Corinthian pillars; an arched relief of a naked man and woman entwined in grape vines ran between them. You could have ridden in on the back of a stallion without bending down.

"Looks like the owners have had themselves replicated for posterity," I said.

"Adam and Eve," Baron replied. "The name of this pile is Paradise. And that's a Roman lintel dating from the time of Emperor Augustus."

"You're shitting me."

"He collects modern art, but older will do just fine, too."

I mashed a mosquito that had landed on the tip of my nose and was rewarded with a red smear on my forefinger.

Lawns manicured as meticulously as a golf course surrounded the chateau. The grass was dotted with sculptures, some of which looked like rusty machine parts lifted from Kotka's abandoned metalworks. One was a crooked brick smokestack, about ten meters high. Some bricks jutted unevenly from the sides.

"Lousy bricklayer," I said.

"It's titled *Ladder to Heaven*," Baron noted.

"Wow. You know that much about art?"

"I can see the nameplate with the binoculars."

A man in a green uniform a couple of shades darker than the lawn emerged from behind the building. At first I thought he was a gardener, but then he raised a walkie-talkie and spoke into it. Before long, a second guy in green approached from the alder grove opposite, accompanied by the biggest dog I'd ever seen; it was pitch black, and I could see its teeth gleaming all the way from our hiding spot.

"Fucking hell," I said.

"You mean the dog?" Baron asked.

"No, the guy walking it."

I snatched the binoculars from Baron. I hadn't been mistaken. It was Hiililuoma, the security guard who had knocked Rust to his death from the roof of the maritime museum in Kotka. For a long time I'd thought the guilty party was another guard, Jere Kalliola; I had hunted and harassed Kalliola for weeks. And he had hunted me. In the end, I killed Kalliola and his boss in an abandoned warehouse where they were trying to drown Smew. It was then I learned that the person responsible for Rust's death was Jere's colleague, Hiililuoma.

Now there he was, with that massive monster of a dog. That's what the hound of the Baskervilles must have looked like right before it mauled its victims to death on the moors or made them drop dead just by being so terrifying. This castle made a great backdrop for a horror story in the making.

"What the hell is that prick doing here?" I muttered.

"Janus has his own security guards."

"Why do you keep calling him Janus?"

"Although his real name is Pavel Putikov, he wants everyone to call him Janus. He never goes by Putikov in public. Janus is the two-faced god of ancient Roman mythology. Benign to his own; dreadful to his enemies. That's what this art collector of yours is like."

"That's fucking wonderful. How do you know so much about him?"

"Janus used our real estate company when he was looking for a house, a summer cottage. He was already looking when you still lived in Kotka and Rust was still alive. He wasn't satisfied with anything we showed him. Then he noticed we also had listings for plots of land nearby where he could build himself the dacha of his dreams. Janus picked a zoned lot east of Kotka, just off the old King's Road, and carried a briefcase full of cash into our office. Our manager cleared his throat and explained that wasn't the way business was handled in Finland; he had to open a bank account and pay via bank transfer. A couple of days later his account was up and running, and Janus had transferred a sum six times the price of the lot to our office's accounts. He wanted to buy all the surrounding lots, too, to make sure he wouldn't have any neighbors too close snooping around."

"Did you guys sell all the land to him?"

"His money is just as good as any Finn's, except it was all cash, no loans. Janus had to sign his real name on the deed and prove his identity. That was the one and only time he's used the name Putikov, to my knowledge."

"What else do you know about him?"

"He uses a helicopter to go fishing."

"Tosses sticks of dynamite into the water, huh?"

"After we completed the sale, Janus invited me and my boss to go fishing with him. There we were, casting lines side by side. Janus kept bringing up monsters as long as your arm. My boss caught a single scrawny perch. I didn't catch a thing. Apparently some diver was below the surface, attaching these behemoths to Janus's hook. When we were done, the helicopter picked us up and brought us back to an informal dinner here at the manor. The manor wasn't completed yet so we dined at a table carried out into the yard. The helicopter had flown into Helsinki while we were fishing and picked up Michelin-rated chef Hans Välimäki, who whipped up a ten-course tasting menu from Janus's catch. When we were done eating, Janus asked my boss if he had enjoyed the meal. My boss said, 'Yes, absolutely.' Then Janus said to Välimäki, 'I didn't care for it myself, but because my guest did, I'll give you a tip.' Then he handed him a five-hundred-euro bill."

"You're shitting me."

"Nope. Välimäki tried to explain something about the composition of flavors, but they packed him into the helicopter and off he went. My boss thought Välimäki was going to be tossed to sleep with the fishes or left on a rock in the middle of the sea with the cormorants, but there he was a couple of days later, cooking on some television program. As evening fell, Janus showed us a brief glimpse of blueprints of the manor he was building. The drawings showed the wine cellar. We even got a little tour."

"So he's got plenty of dough."

"He's used to getting whatever he wants with money. And muscle. Depending on who he's dealing with, he'll use one or the other, and if you disagree with Janus, you disappear. Either on your own or through his inducement. This is only my take, Metro. Officially he's every busi-ness owner's dream customer."

"And this is just his summer cottage?"

"Yes. I didn't quite understand what he meant by 'cottage' during our first meeting. I went on and on about weathered wood finishes and no electricity and how wonderful it is to chop your own firewood and carry in water from your own well and warm your little sauna, and of course you have a heart carved into your outhouse door. It was an easy mistake to make based on Janus's appearance. He's so rich that he dresses in badly fitting jeans and the same sort of pilled flannel shirts with holes at the armpits that my father wears. The last time he got his shoes polished was probably 1984. He doesn't shave very often, and he wears a fanny pack. He digs into it now and again to pull out a little camera so he can take a picture of some duck or piece of driftwood."

"Goddammit, that place is almost as big as Kotka City Hall," I said.

"Oh, it's definitely his summer cabin, not city hall," Baron said. "For instance, there's a wood-burning sauna over there. In that out-building where the smoke is rising."

"There's probably room for a hundred people, with a throne in the middle," I muttered.

Aside from the chateau, there was one long outbuilding that slunk across the grounds like a snake, and three smaller ones at the other end of the property. The smoke Baron mentioned was writhing from one of the small buildings. Round and raised in the middle, it looked like a nomad's yurt.

In this context, *small* was a relative term. The smallest outbuilding was exponentially larger than the apartment where Rust and I had spent our final years together.

The sea was a whole three hundred meters away, so Janus had built himself a saltwater pool stocked with water lilies. There they swayed, in a lily pad–shaped pool.

Hiililuoma and his dog had disappeared into the larger outbuilding next to the sauna.

"That must be the kennel," I whispered.

"Possibly."

The dog that had vanished inside the outbuilding suddenly started barking. Hollow woofs echoed across the grounds. A second, equally deep woof joined in from behind the chateau, before another coal-black dog came into view. It tossed its head from side to side; the guard walking it looked like he was having a hard time holding on. When the giant schnauzer opened its maw, it looked like a human head would fit in nicely.

"I hate dogs," I muttered.

Baron turned to leave. "So don't think of them as dogs. Think of them as horses."

2.2 MILLION

We retreated from the birches at the edge of the property into the deeper shadows of the spruces. We found Vorkuta in some tussocks, picking blueberries. Thanks to his Estonian mother, he had a European Union passport in addition to his Russian one, so he had been able to come to Finland with me without a visa. Evidently mothers really can be useful. Sometimes. Vorkuta held up his purple-stained fingers.

"Everything clear?" he asked.

"Anything but," I said. "There are fucking dogs."

"What kind?"

I gave Vorkuta a brief description.

"OK, so not the good kind," Vorkuta said, shaking his head.

"At least they're not Dobermans," Baron said, raising a thumb.

Since the moment we had reconnected two days ago, he had tried to stay positive and make a good impression. I guess he was trying to make me forget the stunts he had pulled six months ago.

"Giant schnauzers are worse than Dobermans," Vorkuta said. "The Nazis used to sic them on people. Dobermans are shih tzus compared to giant schnauzers. They're the great white sharks of the dog world. They'll rip two pounds of meat from your ribs in one bite."

"Nice."

"I knew a guy who had a giant schnauzer," he continued as we made our way to the car under the shelter of the trees. "He and his girlfriend brought the dog along on a road trip to Poland. A romantic tour of the countryside. Whenever they pulled into a town, the villagers would shut themselves in their houses and refuse to come out as long as the giant schnauzer was in view. The old folks still remembered how their family members and friends had been torn to shreds. They called them the hounds of hell."

"Are they fast?" I asked.

"They have four long legs," Vorkuta said. "You have two."

Baron drove us to Kotka along the back roads. The new four-lane highway gleamed over to the side, trucks and cars flashing along. We went to the tip of Kotkansaari Island, where the old oil harbor used to be. The enormous cylindrical tanks had been towed south across the sea to Estonia; all that was left at the shore were the weblike dock structures the tankers used for mooring. The peninsula had been turned into a park years before and the bulldozed soil was covered by grass now.

I climbed a slope of granite up to the top, where the ruins of a two-hundred-year-old fortress still stood. A lone park bench had been hauled up there. Vorkuta was lagging, studying the plants that were thrusting out of the soil. Baron was huffing up the hill.

"This is why elevators were invented," he said, panting.

"What's this?" Vorkuta asked, shaking soil from the roots of a plant with thick, waxy leaves.

"Sedum," Baron said.

"Can you eat it?"

"No," I answered. "You'll choke and your stomach will explode." This was my stock answer to his botanical inquires.

Vorkuta nibbled at the plant with a thoughtful look on his face. He put one of the tuber-like roots between his teeth and crunched.

"Tastes like potatoes. And radish."

"He does this all the time," I said to Baron. "Let's get down to business before he eats something poisonous and croaks on us."

"Where are you guys staying?" Baron asked.

"I'm not telling," I said.

"You can trust me."

"The last time I trusted you I was almost iced by some security guards."

"How many thousands of times are you going to remind me?"

"Not thousands. Millions."

On a scrap of paper I scribbled down a list of things we needed Baron to get for us. We agreed on the schedule for tomorrow. I had him pull out his cell phone and showed him Banksy's *Ice Rat*; the website of the Berlin auction house still had it listed under Sold. Ten photographs, three full shots, and seven details. Above the images, a bolded headline read:

First Banksy Mural with Certificate of Authenticity

Thanks to the certificate from Pest Control, the price had soared to the record-setting figure of 2.2 million euros. That made *Ice Rat* the most expensive work of graffiti ever sold. Up until now, the priciest Banksy had sold for 1.8 million dollars at a Sotheby's auction in New York in 2007. The name of that work was *Keep It Spotless*; it depicted a maid sweeping garbage behind a canvas painted with a bunch of polka dots.

Stories about the sale of *Ice Rat* had appeared in numerous media outlets, and guesses were being made about the identity of the still-anonymous buyer. The work was presumed to have ended up in the United States, Japan, or China, whose newly wealthy upper class spared no expense as it stocked its cellars with the best French wines and its private collections with Western art.

"Are you sure about this?" Baron asked.

"Fifty percent sure."

"What if it's the other fifty percent?"

"If what you told me is true, we have an escape route," I said. "Is it true?"

Baron grunted and made his way down the granite slope in his suit, weaving between some young people tossing a Frisbee on the lawn. He almost took a Frisbee to the head. I stayed up top with Vorkuta. We gazed out at the cobalt sea opening up before us. Three peaks rose on the horizon. Suursaari Island was out there, forty kilometers away. It used to belong to Finland, but now it was part of Russia.

"You should do some graffiti out at Suursaari," I said to Vorkuta as I waved at Baron.

He didn't see me from behind the wheel; he was too busy weaving out of the little parking lot in his company Audi with the smiling house on the side. Vorkuta and I circled around through the alder brush to the rear of Mansikkalahti Bay. Several boats were tied up in the tiny inlet. A tall post stood on top of the breakwater. Boys were taking turns climbing up a few meters and making long leaps into the water.

We sat in a little gazebo and studied the map Baron had drawn for us. Out of the corner of my eye I watched the boys splashing and screaming. I noticed a girl with dark skin among them; she looked like I did a few years ago. When I was her age, I climbed that same pole and jumped into the same bay, legs flailing. We had competed to see who could jump the farthest. These guys appeared to have a similar competition going. I listened to her cackle as she flew, limbs fanning the air before she splashed into the water.

At that age, my only worry was whether I would win the long-jump competition. Or the dash. Or if I could jump farther into the sea from the pole than any of the boys.

Then came the phase when I wanted to be invisible.

After that, I realized that my name was the only thing I truly owned. No one can ever take my name from me, even if they take my dreams. So I started painting it around town. Maria became Metro. Invisible me became can't-miss me.

A rumble echoed beneath the cackling. Vorkuta pointed out to sea. You couldn't see Suursaari Island anymore; a fat dark cloud had blacked out the horizon.

"Thunderstorm," Vorkuta said.

"They don't normally stop here," I said. "They usually stay out at sea or cross inland."

Vorkuta hurried me on; the kids jumping into the water had glued me to the spot. I had been so fucking pissed when Dad disappeared from our lives and Mom and I got stuck living in Kotka. I was even more furious when Rust was killed. But in between were a few years when I had mostly enjoyed being alive. After a couple of summers of hurling ourselves from that pole into the sea, we moved on to the outdoor swimming pool, where there was a ten-meter diving tower; we hassled the lifeguards all day and jumped so much that it seemed like half the water in the pool was splashing onto the people lolling on the lawn.

But now the kids were leaving. Some of them had bikes. A red-headed boy and the girl with the dark skin jogged alongside the others. She looked like she could easily outrun the boys' heavy bicycles.

"Earth to Metro," Vorkuta called.

We followed the shoreline path to Sapokka and jumped on the water taxi that took us to Lehmäsaari Island, passing the little fortress of Kukouri and Varissaari Island. The taxi pulled in at the dock, where groups of people lounged around bonfires, beer bottles clinking. Someone was splashing in the water on an inflatable crocodile roaring, "Me Tarzan!" to his friends on shore as he strangled his croc. We climbed the path between the pitch-dotted pine trunks, and a minute later ditched the trail. We followed the shoreline, heading toward the sun, which was already slowly setting.

There's nowhere in the world the sun sinks into the horizon as slowly as it does in Finland during summertime. It's glued to the sky. Even when night comes, it refuses to drop.

In the stand of pines that rose at the farthest tip of the island stood a tent I had retrieved from my mother's storage space in Karhuvuori. We had used it when I was a little girl. The tent would leak if you touched the roof while it was raining. As a kid, I thought it was so much fucking fun to press the inside with my forefinger despite being told not to. I loved watching the first drop squeeze through while Mom shrieked. *Don't touch the tent!* belonged to the same class of tempting warning as *Don't tear that!* or *Don't throw rocks at the windows of the abandoned house!*

I bent down and checked the zipper; the thin strip of tape I had left there was still in place. I opened the tent and peeked in: two balled-up blankets and both of our backpacks. The mesh pocket at the end of the tent held two headlamps. We had left four big, worn-out pairs of men's swimming trunks drying on a line, along with a towel of Muhammad Ali smashing an opponent's face, just in case someone stumbled across our campsite. We wanted them to think the tent was inhabited by a quartet of boxers so they'd leave it alone.

"So tomorrow's the day the world comes to an end?" Vorkuta asked.

"Tomorrow's the day."

"That means we still have some time." Vorkuta walked down the shore to chuck bits of bread into the water. The thunder rumbled out at sea and a thick orange gradually coated the western sky, as if someone were spray-painting across it. Looming above it all, the glowing red sun glared like the eye of a dead fish.

96 PERCENT

The next day was even hotter than the previous one. Right from the start, the horseflies waged their angry assault on us. The sea was as smooth as glass, and the water along the shoreline was as warm and cloudy as milk. I waded in, trying to get away from the horseflies, and slid in deeper and deeper. The springs at the bottom created alternating currents of cool and warm water. As soon as I thrust my head to the surface, a horsefly dive-bombed my nose and bit off a chunk.

A single cotton-candy cloud hovered in the middle of the sky, completely still. The surface of the sea was an infinite mirror reflecting this cotton ball. A water strider glided across the mirror without sinking in. Dragonflies buzzed among the horseflies like helicopters. We spent the first hours of the day huddled under the shade of the pine trees, the distant giggles of splashing children occasionally carried across from Kotkansaari Island. The island fortress of Kukouri shimmered in the sun like a fairy-tale castle that was still under construction. Boats and ships of all sizes navigated the waters before us, from rusty tankers to Jet Skis that buzzed among the islands more angrily than the horseflies.

We scrambled back into the water when we saw a massive cargo liner bulldoze past. We went so deep we had to dog-paddle to stay afloat. We waited for the cargo ship's wake, which rolled out in high swells. As it rocked us, it felt like the sea washed away all the bad things that had happened to us.

"Not bad," I panted once I was back on shore, lying faceup. "Despite the horseflies."

"Almost as amazing as Orgosolo," Vorkuta said.

"What's Orgosolo?" I asked, remembering that up in the Ice Cave Alyosha had used Orgosolo as the upload location for a couple of our graffiti videos.

"Paradise for graffiti artists."

"How come I've never heard of it?"

"Because you're an amateur."

The thunder started rumbling out on the horizon again. The heat was weighing on me like a breastplate; sweat was dripping down my sides even though I wasn't even moving. As Vorkuta told me about the time he and Alyosha traveled to Orgosolo his voice crackled at my side, as electric as a radio broadcast.

Orgosolo was a mountain village of four thousand souls located on the slopes of Mount Barbagia in Sardinia. Barbagia took its name from a word for barbarian. The village had been home to shepherds for centuries. Prolonged, vendetta-like conflicts persisted between the village's families for generations; someone from one family might kill someone from another family for a trivial reason, like a sheep coming over and nibbling some grass from their yard, or a tree dropping its leaves on a neighbor's property without the landowner having asked permission on the tree's behalf. But more than anything, the villagers were unified in resisting outside control or any attempt at establishing it. Robbery was allowed when the state or the authorities were the target.

"Robin Hoods," Vorkuta said. "A whole village of them."

"Robin Hoods who assassinated each other."

In the late 1960s, the Italian government decided it was going to set up a military facility on the ancient pasturelands outside Orgosolo—a training ground where soldiers would be shooting live ammunition and where civilians and their flocks would no longer have any cause to set foot or hoof.

The shepherds grabbed their shotguns and decided they were going to let the pencil pushers know what they thought about this idea. A herd of anarchists from Milan showed up in the village to join the protest, and the shepherds welcomed them with open arms. But the anarchists advised the shepherds that they might want to consider using weapons other than the traditional shotguns, bricks, and firebombs, since they would be up against artillery and tanks this time. The anarchists urged the shepherds of Orgosolo to express their opinions by scrawling them on the walls of their village. The anarchists promised they would spread the word around Italy and Europe.

The muttering shepherds picked up their brushes and wrote their thoughts about the corruption of the state and the arrogance of the military. The standoff lasted for years; this was before the Internet, so the anarchists disseminated the images by hand and wrote impassioned articles about the innocent mountain village that the army wanted to wipe off the face of the earth. The lambs were bleating before the bull-dozers, *baa, baa*.

The military base never materialized. The pastures were saved. After painting for years, the shepherds were hooked on their new hobby and kept writing on the walls. Cans of spray paint were now their flamethrowers, from which they issued sharp social commentary.

Vorkuta told me how a couple of years earlier he had traveled to the village with Alyosha by motorbike. It was almost impossible to get there; the spring floods had taken out the bridges. Unless the villagers had taken them out, to keep outsiders away. Vorkuta and Alyosha had curved up the cracked, serpentine roads for kilometers, running into three washed-out bridges. The deep, boulder-filled river ran before them, impassable. As evening fell, they finally managed to pick their way through the river's tributaries to the mountain road that led to the village. At one hairpin turn Vorkuta was startled when he nearly ran into a pair of smoldering eyes. The shepherds had painted a boulder near the village to look like a watchful human figure. The first living beings Vorkuta and Alyosha came across in the village were a horse and the young man riding it who gave them the once-over from under his heavy brows. A cluster of surly old men in berets sat at a street corner, silently eyeing them. Two four-wheel drives rumbled past, carrying village men in camouflage, with shotguns slung across their backs. Every lane was narrow, crooked, and steep. Now and again a door would crack open and a woman in a black dress would scurry out, glancing briefly at them as she hurried on her way.

"It was like some Mafia village where speaking was a crime," Vorkuta said. "But the walls!"

Large murals had been painted on the buildings. One was of New York's Twin Towers collapsing. The war in Yugoslavia was being fought in another. In a third, a raft carrying a load of starving, shipwrecked people drifted toward Manhattan; it read: WE ARE ALL ILLEGAL IMMIGRANTS.

At one spot, motorcycles sped over windows and doors, leaping from one wall to the other. The text advertised: ORGOSOLO, PEACEFUL OASIS.

An old man had been painted on another wall, fixing his keen gaze on passersby and informing them: HAPPY IS THE MAN WHO NEEDS NO HEROES.

Vorkuta's voice grew so faint it was almost drowned out by the buzz of the Jet Skis.

"Everyone was staring at us like they'd be perfectly happy to throw us off the cliff. Night was falling and a mountain wind was blowing down the lanes. It was cold. Lit candles appeared in the windows; we heard shots higher on the mountain, as if war had broken out up there. I knocked on a door next to one of the flickering orange windows. It cracked open, and a single eye stared out at me, the whites a maze of tiny red veins. I explained that we needed a place to stay so we wouldn't freeze. The eye didn't understand my language. A new eye appeared at the crack, lower down. Then came a little finger that pointed at the next door over. It opened up to a barn that, based on the smell, had sheltered every animal in Noah's ark, from skunks to warthogs. We walked our motorcycle into the horse's stall, wrapped ourselves in our blankets, and fell asleep to the sound of gunshots echoing down from the slopes."

"Goddammit," I said, swiping away a horsefly that had gotten caught in my eyelashes. My cursing brought Vorkuta back to reality. He had been in Orgosolo. Now he was back on the shores of Lehmäsaari Island. "Tell me more."

"Some other time. I don't feel like talking about Alyosha anymore."

Changing the subject, Vorkuta claimed he could spot a sea eagle circling overhead. I remained on my back for a long time, focusing on the area where his finger was pointing, but all I could see were dark spots dancing back and forth. Vorkuta said what I was seeing were the knots of my convoluted thoughts.

It was so hot that afternoon that the edges of our shadows blurred; they shimmered and steamed. When I held my arm straight out in front of me, beads of sweat formed on my wrist, like springs welling up from inside the earth. My left ankle swelled from the heat, but it could already take my weight pretty well, and I didn't need a crutch to walk anymore. But the horseflies had nipped at my calves all day, covering them in thin trails of blood.

The thunderhead over the open sea grew bigger and darker. We had brought a canister of drinking water with us, but there wasn't a single drop left.

"Are we leaving the tent here?" Vorkuta asked.

"I don't know if we're coming back."

"Then it can wait here for some other wandering soul."

"I took a tent to a music festival once," I said. "We went to listen to the bands and came back late at night. Someone had taken a shit right in the middle of the tent."

On the floor of the tent Vorkuta arranged pinecones into a heart and the word *welcome*. "Maybe this will help."

"You always have faith in the goodness of humanity."

We crossed the island back to the saltwater pothole where the water taxi stopped.

Crocodile guy was sprawled on the beach, his rubber reptile at his side. He was snoring, and his skin was on fire from the sun. His hand lay in the middle of his chest. The water taxi puttered up, waking him. A white handprint burned against his lobster-red torso. He must have been asleep in that same position for hours.

"You don't have to come, you know," I said to Vorkuta.

"Alyosha would kill me if I didn't," he said with a grunt, stepping onto the water taxi before me.

From our spot on the upper deck we waved at a sailboat gliding past; the people on it waved back. The inhabitants of Kotka always greet each other on the water. But if two people from Kotka happen to pass each other on the street or in a park, they'll both stare at the nearest trash can or storefront or asphalt or pile of dog shit so they won't have to say anything to each other, heaven forbid. At sea, everything is different.

Maybe I should spend the rest of my life at sea.

Once we were back in town we circled around the peninsula and up to the big granite slope at Katariinanniemi Park. This time, we skipped the bench and picked a spot where we had a view of the road winding down to the park. Directly below us stood a brick building that had been completely covered with graffiti. I even recognized one of my own tags, with a tag Rust had done a year ago next to it. Our tags were interlocked. I looked away.

Baron's company car pulled into the parking lot. Vorkuta circled around the top of the hill so he'd be able to keep an eye on it from above. I waited to make sure no one was following the car. When five minutes had passed and no one showed up, I met Vorkuta back at the bench from yesterday.

"See anybody?" Vorkuta asked in a low voice.

I shook my head. Baron was heaving himself up the slope to the top of the rock.

"Couldn't we have met down at the bottom today?"

"I like watching you huff and puff. You've let yourself get out of shape," I said. "You have the stuff?"

"In the car."

We followed him down the slope. Even on this hot summer day Baron wore ironed suit pants, a light blue dress shirt, and a tie. He had left his suit jacket hanging in the car. There was a big wet splotch spreading out from the middle of Baron's back, like a man-made lake bleeding across a map.

"It's so nice and warm," I said to his back.

"Kiss my ass, Metro."

"You never used to swear."

"You used to be a nice person."

Baron climbed into the Audi, closed the doors behind him, and punched on the air conditioning. The trunk opened; Baron had left a big gym bag back there. Vorkuta and I went through the contents: cans of spray paint, three liters of battery acid, juice in a white plastic jug, a funnel, a metal pot, lighter fluid, charcoal, matches.

I slammed the trunk and opened the passenger door. A cool breeze from the Andes hit me.

"Join me for a picnic?"

"I'll leave you to it, my dear princess."

I left Baron grumbling in his North Pole on wheels while Vorkuta and I went over to one of the grill sites dotting the big lawns. I sat on the bench. Vorkuta lit the coals, and I waited for them to get nice and hot, emptying the three bottles of battery acid into the pot. It was almost full. I realized I had left the gloves in the trunk. Even though battery acid is only one-third sulfuric acid it will eat away at your skin and clothes, and it will do it without you noticing. You don't realize that some of it splashed on you until your skin blisters, and you have a hole in your gear.

"Should we get the gloves?" I asked.

"Gloves are for amateurs," Vorkuta said. "Pros have a steady hand."

I couldn't help but laugh. Vorkuta had this thing with his nervous system that made his hands tremble all the time. You couldn't imagine him as a brain surgeon or a diamond cutter, unless you wanted to lose your brains or jewels forever.

He took hold of the pot and lifted it up onto the grate in one smooth motion, not spilling a single drop.

"How'd you do that?" I asked.

"I pictured myself holding a can of spray paint instead of the pot. My hands never tremble when I paint."

We stepped back as the battery acid started boiling and the water evaporated. The acid sputtered over the edges of the pot, and an acrid stench filled the air. Some sausage grillers who had appeared at the next site glanced over at us, frowning. Two of them were skinheads.

"We're boiling some rotten eggs over here," I called over to them. "My national dish. From the Congo. You guys want some?"

"Fucking nigger," one of them said.

"Yeah, and this guy here is Russian. The real deal, a Russki whose grandpa bazookaed your granddads during the war. He has a black belt in karate and systema. You guys ever heard of systema? It's a martial art practiced by Russian special forces. They know how to kill with a pen if they have to. Or charcoal. He's used to kicking Finns' asses. Runs in the family. You guys want to try him?"

"Eat shit and die, Russian lover."

"I can translate that for him, but I'm not responsible for the consequences."

"What are you guys talking about?" Vorkuta asked, unable to understand most of the Finnish.

"The weather. Nasty heat wave."

Vorkuta's eyebrows rose as he watched the trio retreat to a grill at the far end of the park.

"They're afraid of you," I said.

"Me?"

"Yeah, I don't get it either."

We gulped down some juice while we waited for our soup to finish cooking. The sun had warmed the granite during the day, and it felt like the juice evaporated the second I sucked it down, just like the water from the pot. We let the remaining sulfuric acid cool down and then we used the funnel to pour it into the empty juice jug. Boiling down battery acid will get you 96 percent sulfuric acid. I wasn't sure if ours was quite that potent, but it was definitely pretty close.

"Is that plastic going to hold?" Vorkuta asked.

"It did when Rust made this."

We buried the bottles of battery acid, the funnel, and the pot in the garbage can near the grill, and I started walking the sulfuric acid over to the car. I waved good-bye to the skinheads. They gave me the finger.

I knocked on the window of the Audi. Baron looked like he was sleeping in there. He opened the door with his eyes shut, and a bit of glacier smacked me in the forehead. I could almost hear the icebergs grinding against each other. Behind the Audi, lightning flashed above the steaming sea.

"OK, we're ready," I said. "Drive on to the end of the world."

IRON BOOT

Baron headed north. At Hovinsaari Island I glanced back at the yellow Art Nouveau school and the apartment buildings that loomed behind it. Jack, a member of our old graffiti crew, had lived in one of them. Like Baron, he betrayed me. He ended up involuntarily taking the fall for the two guards I had killed. Yup, I framed him.

I didn't have any regrets. Prison was exactly what that traitor piece of shit deserved. I almost slashed his throat with an ice skate blade. At least this way he got to live.

A woman with gray hair was trudging down the street. I wondered if it was Jack's mom. I had never met her. Maybe it was her; maybe her hair had gone gray overnight when her son ended up in the clink.

I pressed my nose to the passenger-side window and realized that I didn't know anything about the parents of my old friends. I had never heard Rust say a word about his parents. I had only grunted something to Rust about Mom and Dad a couple of times. We had excised our pasts.

The highway was packed with long-haul semis; trapped between two of them, our car reminded me of a patty smushed between two hamburger buns. After we passed Hamina, Baron steered toward the old, winding King's Road; it had a single lane to the highway's four. The contrast couldn't have been greater. The thirty kilometers from Hamina to Virolahti Bay was the longest extant stretch of the highway Sweden's king had built in the 1300s between Turku in the west and Viipuri in the east. The narrow road didn't have a single straightaway; it rolled up and down through hundreds upon hundreds of curlicues. The locals did a hundred kilometers an hour in sixty-kilometer zones and cut blind corners. We came across a caravan of motorcycle riders heading in the other direction. They gathered from around Finland to drive the King's Road.

After a few kilometers Baron turned off the King's Road and continued along an even narrower dirt road. He was going to drop us off at the edge of a field, a spot I had picked after consulting a map. We had about two kilometers to our destination from there.

"This is going to cause me problems," Baron said.

"Please," I said. "You're so slippery you'd slither through a shit-clogged drain."

Vorkuta was carrying a plastic alarm clock he had bought for five euros. He set the time to Baron's clock. Vorkuta also had a used burner phone he had picked up; its clock was stuck in on Bangladesh time. We were only planning on using the burner for filming.

We stepped out of the car. Baron held out his hand. I shook it. For a second I was afraid he would try to hug me. I would have kicked him in the nuts.

We watched the rear of the Audi disappear down the forest road. The dust floated in the air for a long time.

"Dust is all that's left of us in the end," Vorkuta said.

"Yup, dust and the stench of sweat."

We walked along the bottom of the ditch that ran along the edge of the angled field, toward a stand of spruces. At one point we came across a clutch of at least ten little frogs packed into a small pool at the bottom of the ditch; they were trying to stay wet and alive surrounded by bone-dry clay. Halfway across the field we stopped and checked the bag. The juice jug hadn't leaked through. Yet.

"It's so fucking light out here," Vorkuta said. "Too light."

The field came to an end at a muddy bank that was pierced by holes. At first I thought they had been made by moles. Then we heard a twittering coming from inside, and a flock of swallows surged out and wheeled overhead.

We climbed into the woods, which turned out to be a bog. The heat wave had dried out the peat and our feet sank into the moss, which was soft, like whipped cream.

We could hear barking somewhere up ahead. We stopped.

"That sounds higher pitched than those black motherfuckers," I said.

We waited. The barking advanced across the woods.

"It's on the loose. It's following someone."

Beyond the stand of trees the thunder rumbled over the water, but the glimpses of sky we could catch above the crowns of the spruces were blue. We walked side by side, dodging the trunks.

"Why is your name Vorkuta?" I asked.

"Why is your name Metro?"

"I wanted to move away from Kotka to a big city where I could take a metro to work."

"Then your dream came true," Vorkuta said and was startled by a hare that bounded out in front of him. "You not only got to ride the metro, you also got to paint them."

"I was supposed to take the metro to the arts academy where I'd study some sort of respectable profession."

"Being a writer is the most respectable profession there is," Vorkuta said. "Why do you need to study and read books? The walls of the city are your books. There's nothing more respectable than spreading your name across walls."

The heat wave had turned the shady thicket into an incubator. Mosquitos whined in our ears as we slogged through the green sauna. The sunlight reached down in narrow strips so sharp they looked like they'd cut your foot in two.

"Vorkuta was a prison camp where they sent deviants," Vorkuta suddenly mumbled at my elbow. "Like gays. And street artists. And people who are too smart for their own good. All of which describe me."

I chuckled and glanced back at Vorkuta. He wasn't smiling.

"For the past three generations, someone from my family has died at Vorkuta."

"Sorry."

"If they catch me, either I kiss my life good-bye or I'll be sent out that way, too. You can always find some suitable penal institution out in Siberia."

"Yeah."

"So I think I'd rather die than follow in my family's footsteps."

A stream meandered through the spruces. We paused on its banks to pick blueberries. The woods were so hot Vorkuta stripped off his shirt. Dozens of mosquitos landed on his back and the three distinct grooves that ran up and down his spine.

"Aren't the mosquitos bothering you?"

"I can't feel anything in my back."

"So the electric shock at the rail yard killed the nerve cells?"

"There never was any electric shock. I got caught once. The police did this."

"What the fuck? That's not what you said before."

"Alyosha wanted to tell a different story."

"They beat you up for painting some piece?"

"No, for being gay. I would have died if it weren't for Alyosha. His dad was working in one of the ministries and raised a huge goddamn stink when they tortured me. His dad got canned for rescuing me, so he kicked out Alyosha. Everyone got the boot. Me first. An iron boot."

Vorkuta turned and showed me a crater between his ribs.

"One of the police kicked me there with his metal-toed boot. Then he wanted me to lick it clean since I had gone and made it dirty."

"Did you?"

"Fuck yes. I licked it when five other cops were whaling on me with chains and batons. Then he kicked my teeth in. Said it's easier for a fag to give blow jobs when he doesn't have any teeth."

THE BUNKER

After a half-hour search, we found the mouth of the bunker under the decaying trunk of a fallen tree. An iron door and a chained padlock prevented entry, but Vorkuta snapped the chain with his bolt cutters. He always carried this essential tool with him on his explorations of abandoned buildings. He'd had to ditch his favorite pair, which he had used for years in Pripyat; they had opened many of the deserted city's secret doors for him.

Baron had drawn us a map. He had spent years surveying all the underground sewers and tunnels in and around Kotka, from the bunkers dating back to World Wars I and II to the later maintenance systems. In his little real-estate-agent mind he held out hope for some future utopia in which humanity would be forced to move underground after a nuclear disaster. He figured he would prepare by familiarizing himself with all subterranean corridors within a forty-mile radius of his home. Baron's bible was Dmitry Glukhovsky's *Metro 2033*; it depicted a globe destroyed by nuclear radiation, where the survivors lived in the metro tunnels of Moscow. Baron was certain our world would be destroyed sooner or later, and he for one intended to be ready to spend the rest of his life in the bowels of the earth. Let everyone else suffer in the marvels of spatial organization and unique floor plans he sold them.

We crouched down and entered the wartime bunker; the walls were damp with moss. Two doors stood at the end of a winding passage; Baron had marked the right-hand one on his map. Apparently the left-hand tunnel dropped down and was flooded with seawater. Baron had explored it years ago by diving twenty meters; the tunnel ended in a chamber where you could breathe stale air that had been trapped for decades.

The right-hand door was steel; blossoms of rust petals covered its surface. A padlock had been looped through the steel hasp years before. Baron had picked the lock when he entered; we didn't need to be so delicate. Vorkuta whipped out the bolt cutters again and clipped the rusted steel hasp from the door.

The passage grew lower and narrower. We made it only ten meters before we hit a spot where it had partially collapsed. We had to crawl past the mound of soil; something buried inside gave off a rotten smell.

After the mound, there wasn't enough room to stand, so we crawled, at times on our stomachs. Tree roots reached down through the ceiling, jabbing at our faces. We had packed our belongings into backpacks. They scraped against the roots; the cans of spray paint knocked faintly against each other. Vorkuta and I weren't carrying our IDs; we had left them in a plastic bag inside a hollow float hanging below the old oil dock in Kotka. If we didn't ever pick it up, our identities would be left to the mercy of the waves.

We heard a clink up ahead. We froze on our stomachs. We heard another clink and then another. The damp penetrated my clothes; my abdomen felt ice cold. The climate underground was totally different from the one three meters above our heads. I figured this was what being in a grave was like, except we could shift positions and move.

I counted the seconds between the clinks. They were regular. Far too regular. I crawled on. Vorkuta held back. I directed my light in the direction of the sound, expecting to get bum-rushed. But it was just a steady drip of water from the ceiling. The drops were falling onto a piece of sheet metal with a clink.

"Are we under the sea?" Vorkuta whispered in my ear from behind.

"The sea's supposed to be that way," I said, nodding to the left. "This has to be some stream above the tunnel. Or a water tank that's leaking."

Vorkuta trapped some water in his palm and licked. "It's sweet."

The tunnel came to an end in a chamber full of rusted-out rails and beams. It looked like a storeroom for train-track construction.

"Baron said there was a plan to build a narrow track here to transport freight inland from the sea. We're close."

"What time is it?" Vorkuta asked.

"It must be past nine."

"Is it light outside?"

"It's always fucking light in the summertime."

Between the stacks of tracks and the wall there was a narrow space you could only squeeze into sideways. The soil was soft and I got dirt in my eyes and under my nails. I wiped spider webs from my face and scraped my knees against the metal rails. In order to fit through I had to hold my backpack down at my side. Deep in the darkness of this narrow gorge there was a tiny cat door at floor level. I flashed my headlamp in so I could see. A square shaft led forward, apparently ending in a rusty wall five meters ahead.

"Baron claims this will take us there. He says there's a right angle in the duct."

"Where it's easy to get stuck."

"I can go first."

"Do you trust Baron?"

"I don't know. But there's no one else I *can* trust at this point."

I shoved my pack into the duct and wriggled in. I turned off my headlamp so its flicker wouldn't attract attention at the other end. The bottom of the duct was cold and wet; I imagined worms crawling into the open neck of my hoodie. I couldn't bend my legs so I had to push off with my toes and then claw myself forward. Luckily I was wearing gloves; otherwise my nails would have snapped off.

After squirming for a few meters I hit the rear wall. I groped left into the darkness. The duct continued that way.

I shoved my backpack left, around the corner. As soon as I had pushed it an arm's length and wriggled in after it I realized I had done something stupid. The duct narrowed past the corner, and the backpack not only slowed my progress but also completely blocked my view.

I tried to pull back but my shoulders caught on the sides. The soles of my feet couldn't find the corner anymore. I tried to spin around and got so confused I couldn't tell if I was facing up or down anymore.

"Goddammit."

Vorkuta touched my ankle. "Problem?"

He had also squirmed into the narrow duct. This was where we would stay forever; our skeletons would be discovered in forty years.

"I can't see anything. My backpack's in the way," I whispered.

"Empty it. Take out enough stuff so you can see over it."

Luckily the flap was facing me. I pulled out cans of spray paint and left them at the side of the duct.

I don't like confined spaces.

I turned on my headlamp for a quick flash.

"There's a metal grille up there," I whispered back.

"I'll hand you the bolt cutters. They're coming up at your right foot."

I reached down behind me and grabbed the cold bolt cutters. I clamped down on a corner of the iron grille. Fatigued as it was by moisture and time, the metal broke easily. After cutting half the bars, I poked at the grille with the cutters. I shouldn't have. The whole grille crumbled and crashed down into the dark space on the other side. The crash seemed to echo for hours.

But there was no shouting. I repacked my backpack and pushed it on ahead of me. That way if someone shot at me, they'd hit my backpack.

Nothing.

I squirmed out through the end of the duct. My knees creaked when I stood. I wiped away the filth that had collected on my face. I took a breath and turned on my headlamp for a second. Hundreds of green cat eyes stared back at me. Wine bottles.

Baron claimed that Janus had no idea the bunker system continued to the other end of the ventilation duct we had just crawled through. The room had several other ducts with iron grilles that looked more or less the same. But those vents led aboveground and were way too small for a person to slip through.

Baron had heard about the bunker system from some ninety-year-old codger who used to work for the government, managing bomb shelters. The duct had been built between the two bunkers primarily for communication purposes; it had never occurred to anyone that a person would try to squeeze through the cramped space. The idea had been to use dogs as messengers if other means of communication were cut off.

The right angle in the duct was necessary in case one of the bunkers was bombed. A straight line would have allowed the shock wave to travel into the other bunker full force.

Vorkuta was now standing by me and had also turned on his headlamp.

"Mouton Rothschild, 1986. This would have been perfect for Alyosha. The same year Chernobyl blew."

"You can take a bottle after we're done," I whispered.

There were doors on either side of the corridor leading out of the wine cellar. Compared to those in the other bunker, these were new, and some of them were locked.

"Baron would cream his pants," I muttered as I counted the doors. Baron had marked on the map that the fourth door from the fire extinguisher would probably be the right one. Even though I had shoved the cans of spray paint into socks they still clinked faintly.

"Are there any surveillance cameras?" Vorkuta asked behind me.

"Not down here, according to Baron."

"How would he know?"

"He got a chance to see the wine cellar that time Janus took them fishing. Baron has been looking for surveillance cameras his whole life. He sniffs them out faster than a truffle dog sniffs out truffles."

"But the building wasn't even completed yet. I'm pretty sure they didn't need surveillance cameras then. If the information your buddy is feeding you is more recent, where did he get it?"

I blushed when I realized Vorkuta was onto something. Baron had contradicted himself. How come it hadn't occurred to me earlier? I scanned all the corners with my headlamp, but all I saw was wine bottles lying horizontally in their racks. There were crates of wine stacked next to the wall.

"What time was Baron supposed to do what he promised?" Vorkuta asked.

"Ten thirty."

Vorkuta glanced at his alarm clock.

"It's ten now."

A FEW FUCKING FLOWERS

At a quarter to eleven we opened the cellar door and climbed up a long, narrow staircase. We found a heavy steel door at the top. There was a handle on our side, so we had no trouble opening it. I cracked it a centimeter. Vorkuta slipped a mirror through the slit; he had snapped it off one of the motorcycles parked at the marina in Kotka.

"Left upper, right upper," he said.

"Can I get at them alone?"

"No. You need me."

"Any smoke coming from the forest yet?"

"I can't see outside."

"Right first."

We burst into the room with the shemaghs covering our faces. I raced for the camera in the right corner. Vorkuta got there before I did and crouched down; I climbed up on his shoulder, one hand supporting myself on his head. He stood, and I sprayed black paint over the camera's lens before I fell. In a flash, Vorkuta was at the opposite corner, waiting for me to get back up on his shoulders. I darkened the second camera.

We scanned our surroundings as we moved forward through what looked like galleries; our headlamps were set to a dim red. The room was full of statues, some still waiting to be unpacked from their big wooden crates. Heavy steel blinds had been lowered across the windows from the outside. There was a small ventilation duct high up on the wall. Vorkuta lifted me up a third time. I saw flashes outside, as if someone were signaling Morse code with a flashlight. I smelled smoke.

"Something's burning somewhere, but I can't see where," I said.

"Do you hear any voices?"

"Some shouting farther off. We should have a little time. Looks like Baron did what he was supposed to."

"There are two more rooms."

We had studied the floor plan Baron had drawn. The windows had alarms, but no one had considered the possibility of anyone except one of Janus's men emerging from the depths of the cellar.

The galleries didn't have the security equipment the big museums used. Here there were no steel doors that dropped down and trapped intruders in a seamless steel can. Janus didn't want any heavy doors between his galleries; he imagined moving through his art collection as a trip down a river into the unknown, a major expedition to the delta of some goddamn river in the Congo. Guests would advance from gallery to gallery along a river projected on the floor. Janus had taken the idea from the Vellamo Maritime Center in Kotka; he wanted to create his own version that was ten times better and included a soundscape featuring the roar of rapids, the lapping of calm waters, the rush of waves, the splash of wading, the cries of waterfowl, the rustling of reeds, and countless other aquatic sounds. *Water is the only material you can cut with a knife, blow up, kick, saw, punch and it immediately heals itself,* Janus had told Baron during the fishing trip. Sound engineers from a couple of universities and the multimedia artist Marita Liulia were preparing the multisensory river projection for Janus.

Or so Baron had explained to us. The multimedia piece wasn't ready yet. Silence filled the galleries.

The middle room was full of wooden crates, too, only a few of which had been opened.

I darkened the cameras in there also.

"We've been here three minutes," Vorkuta said.

When you're trespassing and writing graffiti, every second counts.

There was nothing in sight big enough to be the work transported from Berlin.

We moved into the last gallery. The wall snaked like a river, and you couldn't see the far end of the room. I had the unpleasant feeling that someone was trying to lure us deeper into the serpent's nest.

Vorkuta's shoulders creaked when I jumped up on them to black out the cameras in this room. Sturdy steel blinds also covered the windows of this gallery. We were moving around in the reddish glow of our headlamps.

As we darkened the second camera, I caught sight of Banksy's *Ice Rat*. It had been lifted onto an iron pedestal and was backed by a stout steel plate and heavy struts that prevented the wall from falling backward.

It would have been possible to peel the work from the surface of the wall the way they did with Renaissance frescos, but Janus had wanted to keep the wall to give the impression that *Ice Rat* was from the streets. The surface of the work had been cleaned of filth, fingerprints, and stains, and Ice Rat sliced through the bills on his skates more clearly and brightly than I had ever seen him before. The golden watch on the wrist rising out of the icy water was like the halo of a saint in an icon. Several thin, nearly invisible layers of protective varnish had been applied to the cleaned piece to make further marks impossible.

"Did they use Polycrylic or Soluvar or something else?" Vorkuta asked, shining his light on *Ice Rat* and sniffing it.

"I could give a crap."

It had occurred to me before that paint alone wouldn't do any good. You could always remove paint. I pulled the juice jug out of my backpack and exchanged the cork for the nozzle of a plant mister. I put on a dust mask and protective goggles under my shemagh. I held my breath as long as I could and moved quickly, from right to left and from top to bottom. Then I stepped back for a second and gasped for breath. I didn't want any of the 96-percent sulfuric acid mist inside me.

"Grow, my little flowers, grow," Vorkuta said off to my side, filming me with the cell phone that thought it was still in Bangladesh.

Destroying *Ice Rat* took only a few minutes. Even then, the familiar sensation crept into my guts halfway through: I was too slow; someone was going to catch us. I still made sure not to rush. I sprayed every inch of the piece. Three times over.

"Master gardener Metro," I muttered as I backed up and watched the surface of the work bubble and blister. "Restore that, fuckers, and you're smarter than Einstein."

"Look what we have here," Vorkuta said. He reached behind *Ice Rat* and walked over to me, carrying a plastic pocket. Inside was the Pest Control certificate of authenticity. The half of a ten-pound note Verboten had mentioned was attached to it, bearing the handwritten serial number BY00000001.

"Hand me the lighter and keep filming," I said.

I held the certificate of authenticity up in front of *Ice Rat*, read the Pest Control certificate and the serial number out loud, and lit it from a bottom corner.

"Bye-bye," I said to the flames, and then I scattered the ashes around.

Vorkuta crouched down in the corner and opened two wooden crates. He pulled out a painting of sunflowers from one of them. "Have you ever seen this in person?"

"My mom has a bath mat like that."

"This is by that crazy Dutch guy who chopped off his ear. His room was so drab he painted a few of these sunflower pictures to brighten it up."

"Looks like something Mom would make," I said.

"He couldn't afford to buy flowers. That's why he painted them. No one bought them during his lifetime. Nowadays this is worth over a hundred million dollars. If anyone was crazy enough to sell one."

"You're shitting me."

"There are a few versions of this. The others are in museums, but one is in a private collection. The owner is some anonymous millionaire."

"Anonymous no more."

I stared at the sunflowers bursting from the huge vase for a minute, then sprayed my extrastrength sulfuric acid over the hot yellow petals. I watched as saffron and orange dripped down the canvas; the color bubbled and boiled silently.

"That's a goddamn Van Gogh," Vorkuta cried out.

"If no one else gets to see this, then Janus doesn't, either. It's a cheap price to pay for Smew's and Alyosha's lives. A few fucking flowers."

I gave the painting another squirt of sulfuric acid, corked the juice jug, and slipped the jug into my backpack.

Then I pulled out a can of spray paint.

ELECTRICITY

We headed back through the gloomy serpentine galleries. Surrounded by so many crates of various sizes I felt like I was walking through the Jewish memorial in Berlin; you get a sense of your own insignificance among its three thousand or so slabs of poured concrete. At times the path there dips below ground level, and all you can see between the slabs is a slender strip of sky, the clouds racing across it like greyhounds.

A protective coating similar to the one used on *Ice Rat* was applied to the surface of the slabs at the Jewish memorial so no one could scrawl permanent tags on them. They're afraid some neo-Nazi would get the bright idea of marking them up with swastikas.

I shook the image from my head; I had to concentrate. Vorkuta had already slipped though the cellar door and was waving at me to follow.

At that instant, the entire building shook with a powerful rumble; brilliant light flashed through the paper-thin slits in the steel blinds, as if someone were shining an air-raid spotlight. I freaked out and jumped backward. Vorkuta did, too, and the door between us clicked shut.

The lights in the galleries came on.

I grabbed the cellar door and pulled. It didn't budge.

"Open it!"

"I'm trying," I heard from the other side.

A rumble behind me. I glanced over my shoulder. The steel blinds in front of the picture windows had started to rise.

"Open it, goddammit. The lights are on and the blinds are opening!"

"It's security-locked. The electric system." Vorkuta's pounding echoed from the cellar side of the door. "Goddamn steel bars suddenly sprang out of the sides."

By now the blinds had risen to knee height. The world was rumbling and flashing; as we made our advance through the tunnel, the thunderstorm had come in from the sea and parked directly overhead. The lights in the galleries flickered on and off; my eyes couldn't properly adapt to the darkness before I was blinded again.

The glow I had spied through the ventilation duct hadn't necessarily been a forest fire. It could have been the flash of lightning.

I yanked the handle.

"Open it!"

"It won't open!" I heard from the other side. The door thudded; Vorkuta was kicking it.

I crouched down. It was hard to see out because the midday glare suddenly popped on inside again. I felt like an object on display; the only thing missing was a sign around my neck. Then the lights went dark. Lightning split across the grounds and for an instant I could make out the rain-lashed lawn. No forest fire would ever stay lit out there, regardless of whether or not Baron had done what he was supposed to. The plan had been for him to light a fire at ten thirty.

The forest-fire idea felt totally stupid now. The intent had been to divert the security guards away from the outbuildings by giving them a fire to extinguish.

"I'm sorry," I heard from the other side of the door. "I gotta go. The lights in here are turning off and on, too. Someone might come."

Vorkuta banged the steel door three times in farewell; after that, dead silence.

I advanced from crate to crate at a crouch, trying to stay out of sight. A siren was blaring at the perimeter of the property. The steel blinds were at chest height now. The floor beneath my feet shivered from a fresh rumble of thunder. Rain pelleted the lawn, tearing into it.

There was a door to the outside at the end of the first gallery. It faced the main building, but I didn't have a choice. I turned the handle.

It stayed as firmly locked as the cellar door.

I jiggled the handle; nothing happened. The thunderstorm had screwed up the entire electric system.

It was hard to concentrate when the room around me was constantly plunging into total darkness and then shining with bright spotlights, and switching back and forth.

I knocked over one of the upright crates in the first gallery; the statue inside banged against the sides. I barely had the strength to hoist it up so I could use it like a battering ram. I stumbled toward the window and smashed the crate into the glass. It didn't leave the tiniest mark. The floor shook, but that was from the thunder reverberating, not my ramming.

A siren started wailing at the other end of the grounds, died out, and wailed again.

I gathered speed all the way from the opposite wall and crashed the bottom of the crate into the window again. The glass went gray at the point of contact, splintering and creating a mosaic. The lights popped back on, and I was standing there, holding the crate in my arms like a runway model in the glare of the spotlights.

With the third smash, the splintering spread. The surface of the window had turned into an impenetrable web. It was bulletproof; it had a layer of either aluminum or ultrastrong plastic between the sheets of glass. It wasn't going to be broken by me.

The darkened surveillance cameras buzzed overhead like a swarm of bees, desperately seeking out their target.

I crouched down behind a crate near the door. There were only two exits in the winding, three-room gallery. One led to the cellar; the other one led out. Both of them were locked.

The ventilation ducts were so small that even if I were able to rip off the steel mesh I wouldn't be able to fit more than an arm inside.

The lightning flashed and the thunder growled, but there were a few seconds between the flashes and rumbles: the storm was moving away. The steel blinds were completely raised now. I kept imagining a dark, broad-shouldered figure moving through the rain, but then the downpour would tear the vision to shreds.

Getting hurt isn't the worst thing in the world. The worst thing is waiting for someone to hurt you. The longer you have to wait, the more horrible it is.

I thought about Rust; I had a hard time envisioning his face these days. I had sworn I would never forget him. I remembered what his handshake felt like, how happy he had been to hold me in the middle of the night, lying in bed or outside in the darkness, hiding from security guards in the bushes or next to a train car waiting for the right moment to run. Rust would wrap his arm around the part of me that was hurting: sometimes my thigh, sometimes my arm, sometimes my side, sometimes my neck.

When I felt his squeeze, I didn't have to be afraid.

I squeezed my own thigh. It didn't do any good. My heart hammered in my chest more violently than the thunderstorm.

I tried both the cellar door and the outside door one last time. Neither one budged.

I waited. And waited.

I wished that Dad were next to me right now, that he'd take me by the hand and say, "Maria, everything's going to be fine."

A black car had crushed the life out of Dad. It was me they were trying to kill, not him. They had made a mistake; Dad had been wearing my leather jacket. I was responsible for my father's death.

Revenge was the only thing that was keeping me alive.

I waited. I got tired of waiting. Didn't it occur to those idiots in the security station to come check why the monitors are all black?

Suddenly, it felt like I didn't have a single bone in my feet.

When I know something is about to go down, all the strength drains out of me. I used to get the same feeling before meets at my track-and-field club. Before the signal for the hundred meters my legs would soften into cooked spaghetti in the starting blocks; the slightest breeze would knock my knees out from under me. Then the starting gun would ring out in the stadium, and I would bolt forward, charged by electricity.

I heard muffled voices outside the door. They must have been talking really loudly for their voices to carry through the steel and the thunderstorm. Someone was turning the door handle; I could see it move.

A click. A key had been inserted into the lock.

The door opened a crack. A flashlight appeared inside, then a hand, then an arm in a green sleeve.

I aimed low, plowed the guard out of my way, and ran like the little girl on that red-rubber track all those years ago. Pain shot through my left ankle with every footfall.

I didn't care.

LONG LIVE METRO!!!

I flew past two dark figures. It was less than a hundred meters to the forest.

It was hard to stop myself from looking behind me.

The rain felt like someone was whaling on me. The lawn had turned into a waterlogged swamp that sucked my feet down. It was like I was running in a pot of glue steaming with lard and internal organs.

Someone behind me was bellowing.

I ran like that kid did during her races. I stayed focused on what the coach had pounded into my head. *Don't look to the side, don't look back. Relax. Relax. I'm electricity, I'm electricity. I don't have to do anything. I don't even have to breathe. A hundred meters is such a short distance I won't need to draw a single breath.*

My competitors are going to fall back, step by step. Their panting will recede. Their legs will tighten up as they panic and try to catch me. The harder they try, the stiffer their stride will become. They'll tense themselves and their pace until both break. Their panting is receding.

But for some reason I heard the panting behind me grow louder and closer until it drowned out the downpour.

An invisible force knocked me over; water sprayed up as I tumbled across the lawn.

A heavy black storm raged on top of me. Suddenly my hand hurt like hell. I screamed.

Teeth flashed before my eyes; they were going for my throat. I tucked my chin to my chest and rolled onto my side. Now my leg was being torn out of its socket.

"That's enough, Suski. Good girl, good girl," said a voice from overhead.

"Josie, release. Release!"

The pressure on my leg and hand eased off. I was lying in a puddle with my heart pounding, the rain whipping my face. The heads of two black dogs growled less than two meters away. They heaved their slobbering mouths from side to side; their teeth glittered in the beams of flashlights. I could see my own blood on their teeth.

"Where are you off to in such a hurry?" asked a steely voice.

There were three men. Two giant schnauzers, three men. The flashlights turned the rain into a blinding kaleidoscope.

"The lightning scared me," I mumbled.

"I can't hear you!"

"The lightning scared me! I was in the forest!"

I shouted all this; there was a particularly long rumble. I held my thigh. The beam from the flashlight swept across it; a red splotch was forming through the torn pants.

"So why did you pop out of that building, then? If you were in the forest."

"I was looking for a place to get out of the rain."

I started sobbing; I shivered and tried to look as miserable as possible. It wasn't difficult, soaking wet with a dog bite in my leg.

"Goddammit, no one can get in there. The door's locked."

"It was open. I swear it was open. I'm afraid of thunder and lightning. You're not supposed to go near trees, and there were trees everywhere."

"What do you mean, open?" the voice asked. "What you're telling me doesn't make any sense!"

"I was picking blueberries and I got lost and then it started raining and I huddled under a spruce to get out of the rain and then the lightning started and I got scared that the lightning would hit me too and I started running and lightning split a tree next to me in half and I ran and ran and I was totally panicking and then I saw a light up ahead. There was a building with lights on in the middle of the forest. It was that building. The blinds in front of the windows started coming up and I could see the light behind them and I thought there must be someone inside since the blinds were coming up. I rushed over so I could get out of the rain. Another bolt of lightning hit really close. The door opened. I ran in. The electricity kept turning off and on. Then when I tried to get out the door was locked."

"She's totally freaked out," another voice said.

"Sounds plausible to me."

"This is private property," said the metallic voice.

The thunderstorm drowned out some of what they were saying. The flashlight beams were relentless; they wouldn't release me.

"It's raining so hard," I said and sobbed so loudly they would all hear me. "I don't know where I am. I'm sorry. I was scared!"

"Hey, there's no problem. Just take it easy."

"Why did those dogs bite me?" I sobbed.

"They didn't bite you that badly. It was an accident. You shouldn't have run from them. They got a little excited. If they really meant to bite you, you'd feel it."

"I want to go home," I wailed. "I was so scared I lost my phone in the woods."

"Yeah, yeah, take it easy. You're fine."

"We need to check those electrical systems," said one of the guards, as if I wasn't there. "It's not the first time they've acted up. The cameras died as soon as the thunderstorm approached. We have to be sure they won't short every time it rains. The concrete pour is defective. We have to get it fixed right away, before they hang the art and throw that party."

"I thought the wiring was installed underground."

"Yeah, but the transformer is over there, completely unprotected."

"It has a lightning rod."

"It doesn't seem to be doing any fucking good in this weather."

"I want to go home!" I shrieked.

"Yeah, yeah, one of us can give you a ride. But remember for future reference that this area is off limits. This is private property."

"I didn't know." I howled, holding my leg. "I got scared. My dad was killed by lightning! I don't even know where I am." For a second I considered crying and saying I was bleeding to death. "Where's the car? I want my mommy. She's probably worried."

"Go toward that round building. The car is right around the corner from it."

"A round building doesn't have any corners," one of the voices said and chuckled.

"You know what I mean, Einstein."

"I just don't want her to get lost again looking for a corner on a round building. Janne, why don't you take her over."

Laughter erupted around me. It was high time to get out of there. I struggled to my feet; the giant schnauzers on either side of me growled. One of the guards, evidently Janne, headed off with me. I limped slowly toward the round building looming ahead.

"Look, the lights are still going on and off," one of the guards said behind me. "There must be a short in the electrical system."

"I said the blinds and locks should be on separate systems," the third one shouted, trying to make himself heard above the rumbling sky.

"You want to roll them up and down every evening and morning like some fucking organ grinder?"

"Hell, no, but they should have a dedicated system. Separate from the rest of the network."

I limped a little faster when the two guards behind me slowed down to argue and Janne slowed down to listen to them. Maybe there would be a key in the ignition and I'd be able to drive off. Or if I made it to the edge of the forest I'd have a chance then, too.

"Hold up," I suddenly heard behind me.

"What the hell!" the metallic-voiced guy bellowed.

"Stop! Stop!"

I picked up the pace.

"Suski, stop thief!"

One of the giant schnauzers ran out in front of me, blocked my way, and let out a deep growl. Teeth as sharp as the ones in the dog's mouth seemed to be shooting down from the sky. I slowly turned around. The other giant schnauzer was right next to me, its quivering maw agape, as if deciding whether to close its jaws around my thigh, my arm, or my throat.

The guards' heads were swiveling between the gallery building and me. The lights that had come on in the final gallery revealed the greeting I had sprayed there.

METRO WAS HERE!!!

ICE RAT IS DEAD!!!

LONG LIVE METRO!!!

EBOLA

I was being dragged by the hair, stumbling and slipping across the wet lawn. One of the guards yanked me into the galleries through the door at the end of the building. The LED lights still weren't working properly; their intensity fluctuated as if we were walking through deep waves and were catching only intermittent glimpses of the bright sky.

"You're that goddamn Metro," the guard with the metallic voice said up ahead. It was Hiililuoma. I had no trouble recognizing him now that we were inside. "You're the one who harassed Jere to death."

"I didn't harass anyone."

Hiililuoma whacked me in the chest with his metal flashlight. I dropped to my knees.

"Bring her here."

The third guard, the one whose name I didn't know yet, dragged me along the floor, past packing crates, and into the middle room. Hiililuoma and Janne, holding back both giant schnauzers, followed us in.

"Leave them outside!" the third guard ordered.

"It's raining out there."

"Exactly! If they shake off in here the art is going to get drenched."

"Should I tie them up?"

"Why don't you try figuring that out yourself? Rannikko, bring that bitch over here. She's the one who killed Jere."

"What the fuck?" Rannikko shouted in my ear.

"I didn't kill him."

Hiililuoma whacked me with the flashlight again, this time in the temple, before saying, "Did anyone ask you anything?"

I collapsed. My head would have crashed into the floor if Rannikko hadn't been holding me by the hair.

"First this bitch Metro paints Jere's car, then she paints his family's house, then she spreads lying bullshit posters about Jere all over town, accusing him of being a murderer. Jere almost lost it. You guys knew him; the guy could take just about anything. Except for constant harassment and torture and everything that mattered to him being destroyed one thing at a time. Then Metro here paints Jere's house a second time so Jere's wife has a miscarriage, and in the end she fucking kills Jere. She also killed Raittila, slit his throat like some goddamn Arab terrorist."

"This bitch?" Rannikko said.

"Yeah, and the wrong guy is doing time for the two murders. She arranged that, too."

"What?"

"Yeah, Ismo fucking Hietanen. He was one of our guys. A lazy shit, lived with his mom and did some menial job at a warehouse. One of those guys who's been told what to do his whole life. He never would have been capable of mounting any sort of sustained assault himself. He was our informant on the stainer crew."

"You killed Rust," I rasped. "You're the one who started all this."

"Do you guys hear whining?" Hiililuoma said. "Are the dogs still inside, goddammit?"

"You knocked Rust down from the roof of the Maritime Center," I said as Hiililuoma waved the flashlight in front of my face.

"Oh yeah, I remember Spider-Man. He fell from that roof all by himself. He lost his grip, poor guy. His arms were like wet noodles. Climbing where he shouldn't have been."

"I saw the whole thing."

"What did you see, supposedly?"

"I was in the boat and I saw. I just didn't know who it was. The killer. You or Jere or your boss. I saw you knock Rust down with your baton."

"This is exactly what they're like," Hiililuoma said, laughing as he spoke to Rannikko, who was still pulling me up by my hair. "Can't stop lying. They have some sort of Munchausen syndrome. They believe their own lies and their sick truths. This is what spawns mass murderers, like that guy in Norway. Or else they head off to the Middle East to be terrorists. Their biggest dream is to strap on a bomb and blow up a school full of kids. Don't let her looks deceive you."

"You killed him."

"Say one more word and I'll kick your teeth in," Hiililuoma growled. "You'll speak when you're spoken to."

I shut up and lay there with my head still held up by Rannikko. The floor swayed; I felt like vomiting.

"Here before you, you see a mass murderer. This is what they're like. Pests. This is what the Ebola virus looks like in human form," Hiililuoma said, grabbing my ear and twisting my face toward his. "Your real name isn't Metro. What is it?"

"Express," I croaked.

He whacked both of my ears.

"What the fuck did you do here, you goddamn Ebola?"

"There was lightning. I was afraid."

"You know what happens to liars?"

I closed my eyes and steeled myself to take another blow or a kick.

"Rannikko, hold her. I'm going to have a look in the other room."

For a moment it was quiet. I was hoping he wouldn't notice. I thought about Rust, about him falling. This must have been how the long drop felt, even though he plunged thirty meters to the asphalt in a couple of seconds.

A roar exploded from the other room. "Motherfucker! Fucking, fucking, fucking fuck!"

My head lurched as Rannikko took a step toward the last gallery. My weight was a brake, and he let me go. He wanted to know.

I glanced back at the door leading outside. The third guard, Janne, was standing between it and me. Why did they call this guy by his first name? Maybe he was nicer than them? Who knows? All I did know was that he was rocking back and forth, along with everything else. I bit my cheeks so the rocking would stop. The walls swayed; the ceiling was alive, a billowing sea.

Someone kicked my back, and the rocking stopped. An unbearable burning tore through my body, as if I had been thrown into a bonfire.

"What have you done, whore?"

My body absorbed even more kicks. I couldn't breathe, even though I gasped for air, mouth wide.

"Answer me! Now you have permission to answer!"

I still had my backpack on, and he wrenched it off me. It was blocking some of his kicks. The shoulder straps were tight, and I flew backward. Hiililuoma dragged me across the floor.

"Hey, be careful," Rannikko said.

"Because of this Ebola?" Hiililuoma said, laughing. "I promise she's not contagious."

"No, the art. So you don't ruin it."

"Oh, yeah."

Hiililuoma took a deep breath and a couple of steps backward. I finally managed to drag in a breath though my body felt like jelly. I heaved as if I had been underwater for many minutes.

"It's hard getting blood off canvas," Rannikko added.

"Are you a painter or something?" Hiililuoma growled. "You seem familiar with the technical details."

"I've gotten blood on my clothes a few times. It's really tough to get out."

"Syphilis Lips here has destroyed the new work that was just brought in."

"Which one?" Janne asked from his station by the door.

"The wall. I told them they shouldn't bring graffiti here. It just attracts Ebola."

"We don't make the decisions about acquisitions."

"We don't? No shit? I had no idea."

Hiililuoma clenched his hand into a fist. Rannikko was now seriously curious about what was in the last gallery. He twisted both of my arms painfully behind my back and pushed me forward. Blood from my nose dripped to the floor.

"Look," Hiililuoma said, dangling my backpack right above the floor like a sack of stones.

"That's the rat piece?" Rannikko said.

"It fucking was."

Out of my peripheral vision I could see that the destruction was absolute. There was nothing left of the original rat but an amoeba-like blob on the wall; the ice-blue paint had partially melted to the floor. The surface of the wall was as full of gouges and craters as a teenager's face. The banknotes that had covered the surface of the ice had spread into green blotches that looked like tadpoles. The only thing left of the banker's top hat was a splotch of ink.

"How's Janus going to like it when he finds out you destroyed his piece?" I said.

"Us? You're the one who did it," said Rannikko. "And that means big problems for you."

"Neglect. Serious neglect," I spat out before a new kick from Hiililuoma made contact. I managed to shift enough so his shoe hit my shoulder and chest instead of my face.

"Janus isn't going to like this one bit," Janne said from behind me. "How the hell are we going to get that fixed?"

"Neglect," I said. "You'll get fired. You'll end up on the blacklist."

Hiililuoma kicked again. This time my feet went out from under me. You'd think you would stop feeling kicks after receiving so many. Wrong. They hurt like someone's ripping your limbs out of their sockets. I hoped I'd lose consciousness as fast as possible.

"There's another ruined one over here," I heard through a hazy red veil as one of my eyes was swelling shut.

"Goddammit!"

Rannikko dragged me across the floor. The orange-and-yellow canvas was in front of me on the floor. Hiililuoma was shouting words in my ear that I had a hard time understanding.

"Fix it!"

I finally understood.

"What?"

"Fix it. Them. Both of them."

"I can't."

Hiililuoma kicked me in the back.

"Hey, calm down," Rannikko said.

"Shut up."

"She can't fix anything if you kick her to death."

"You have five minutes."

I started to laugh amid the agony. Did Hiililuoma seriously imagine I'd be able to do anything in five minutes, let alone restore what I'd destroyed? Then I realized that's what he was used to. Writers snuck into rail yards at night, painted the side of a boxcar in an instant, and then sprinted back into the darkness. Or painted a whole wall in a few minutes. He knew as well as we did that every minute doubled your chances of getting caught. But it's a totally different thing when you do a carefully considered project. You can easily spend a whole day, a whole weekend, on a piece if you're painting in a peaceful spot where you don't have to worry about taking a boot to the kidneys, pepper spray to your eyes, or a baton to your solar plexus.

Five minutes to fix Banksy and Van Gogh? I knew that if I uttered one word in protest I'd be beaten to death on the spot.

"Backpack," I said in a hoarse voice.

"If you try anything I'll kill you," Hiililuoma said. "I'll let the dogs rip out your guts."

"Hey, hey, come on," Janne said.

"Hey, hey, hey," Hiililuoma answered. "Why don't you go home and give that blonde wife of yours a hug. Your shift just ended. Rannikko, bring Suski over here. For a little motivation. Josie can stay outside."

The schnauzers' ordinary names somehow made them more frightening. I wished they had been called Killer and Fang.

Hiililuoma shook out the contents of my backpack.

"A single wrong spray and Suski will let you know what she thinks about it, with her teeth."

The giant schnauzer growled in my ear. She had eaten something half-rotten and was breathing the hot smell of dug-up carcass in my face.

"Suski likes to hunt down her own prey. Isn't that right, Suski?"

The giant schnauzer howled in my ear, casting her dark shadow over me.

"You have five minutes. Thirty seconds are already gone."

I picked the blue paint, gave the lake Ice Rat was skating across a fresh coat. I immediately saw how pointless this all was. There was still acid on the surface, and it ruined the color the instant it came into contact with the wall. The same thing happened with the white. Banksy's rat was nothing but a shapeless splotch that I hopelessly tried to contour.

"There are bloodstains all over the floor," Rannikko noted.

"Ebola can wipe them up with her own clothes. Then she can wash the windows."

I sneezed; blood flooded into my mouth.

"Three minutes are gone," Hiililuoma said. "You're making colossally bad progress."

It didn't make any difference to Hiililuoma. He knew I wouldn't be able to finish this. He didn't give a shit about the whole thing in the first place. He just wanted to humiliate me. The giant schnauzer growled whenever I moved my foot the tiniest bit.

"Can I grab a sip of juice?" I croaked.

"Drink all you want. You'll be puking it all up in a second. If you're not finished in one minute you're going to get an ass-kicking like you wouldn't believe."

I fumbled among the cans of spray paint for the juice jug, twisted open the cork, raised it to my lips. But I didn't drink. Instead, I flung the leftover sulfuric acid into the eyes of the giant schnauzer growling at my side.

THE CHOPPING BLOCK

I had a second longer than the guards; they didn't know what was in the jug. As soon as I flung the acid I dove behind the nearest crate. In its fury, the giant schnauzer would blindly attack whoever was closest.

"Suski! Heel! Suski!" one of the three guards—I couldn't tell which one—roared amid the howling. I scrambled away from the commotion. The yelping and shrieking were deafening, and it was hard to tell which sounds were coming from the dog and which ones were coming from her victim. Suddenly, the very clear cry of a man erupted from the chaos; it sounded like a saw blade cutting into flesh.

"Kill her!"

"Heel! Suski!"

The room was still rocking and swaying. I followed the winding floor and crawled into a wall. I had headed in the wrong direction; I was at the end of the gallery where there was no exit. I sank down behind a crate.

Crashes mingled with all the other noises, and the other giant schnauzer started barking outside. I heard crying and shouting, then a smash, then the sound of something tearing.

But the most horrible thing was the sudden silence, so heavy it made my eardrums ache.

I waited. I warily peeked out from my hiding place.

I couldn't see anyone. I squatted down and moved closer, staying hidden behind the packing crates.

Someone was panting.

Blood flowed from behind one of the crates, looking like a finger beckoning me, coaxing me to come.

I crawled forward.

I saw a man in a green uniform sprawled on the floor. Blood, smeared with pawprints and handprints, was pooling around him, as if a can of paint had been tipped over.

The dog was a couple of meters away. Her teeth were bared and her head hung to one side. The acid had eaten at her eyes, leaving them a filmy gray. One of her rear legs twitched slowly. Janne was crouched over at the dog's side. He was breathing heavily, as if his mouth were stuffed with coarse felt. He stared ahead, unseeing; he held a bloody baton in his hand. The ceiling lights crackled.

I crept soundlessly behind Janne.

Blood had spurted onto the nearby crates. Suski's rear leg was ticking like a metronome.

When I was right behind Janne's back, I heard sobs underneath his heavy breathing. The guard on the ground was Rannikko. His throat had been ripped out.

Suski had killed Rannikko.

Janne had killed Suski.

I didn't see Hiililuoma. I hoped he was also lying in the shadow of an upturned crate after getting the Suski treatment. Or that he had run off.

Some of the sulfuric acid had splattered onto my jacket, burning holes on the sleeve, as if giant moths had fed on it.

"It's OK, it's OK," Janne kept saying.

I couldn't tell if he was talking to the dog or to his dead colleague. Outside, the rain was still coming down. The lights in the gallery flickered on and off.

When I glanced back at the window, I saw a man with a bloody hand standing in the rain. I backed away from the glass before he could notice me.

I backed right up into Hiililuoma's arms. It was his reflection I had seen in the window, not him. He whacked the back of my head, and my eyes dimmed. He dragged me by my arm into the middle gallery, and then to the first one, ordering Janne to follow; he didn't care how many crates or unpacked statues we bumped into anymore. We passed the window I had tried to shatter earlier; the surface looked like a blizzard.

"What happens to thieves?" Hiililuoma asked me. "What the fuck did you do back there?"

He repeated these two questions, but I don't think he really expected me to answer. Janne didn't answer, either. He walked at my side, his face pale; the tiny drops of blood that had spattered onto it were like nettle rash. Now we were outside. The lawn was as slick as an icy hillside. The thunder and lightning were still filling the sky; we were about to get a fresh cloudburst. The reserve generator was maintaining the yard lights, more or less, but it wasn't producing enough power for constant, steady light, and the outdoor lights flickered like glowworms in the drumming rain.

"What the fuck did you do?" Hiililuoma said, pushing my left hand out in front of me.

Suski had torn a gash in his arm at the elbow, and the rain mingled with the blood until his whole arm was dyed pink. A hundred years ago, when I had lain in wait on the roof of Hiililuoma's row house after Rust's death, I had admired his wife's shirt. His arm was now the same soft pink as that shirt.

"What happens to thieves?" Hiililuoma said again.

I didn't answer, and neither did Janne. The thunder, sounding like a gigantic dog, rolled out from the darkness, joined by Josie's echoing woof. It felt like she was constantly on the verge of pouncing on me.

Hiililuoma hurled me to the ground. I felt something rigid poke me in the back, then something else, and then Hiililuoma hauled me up again. I was surrounded by firewood. He punched me again and pulled me onward.

"Hold her in place. Put all your weight on the Ebola so she doesn't move," Hiililuoma ordered Janne.

I was on my hands and knees. Janne pressed something hard and angular into my stomach as Hiililuoma stretched out my arm in front of me.

"My hand. You destroyed my hand," Hiililuoma said in my ear, and then the sound faded. Maybe he was shouting right next to me the whole time and my spinning brain was just rocked by a beating that felt like it had been going on for hours.

"What happens to thieves?"

Janne mumbled, "It's OK."

The lashing rain momentarily swept aside my profound disorientation. I was on my knees; Hiililuoma was standing in front of me. He had my right hand in a firm grip; my right arm was stretched across a chopping block, its surface scarred by the sharp gouges of axe blades.

Hiililuoma held an axe in his right hand.

He twisted my arm out straight and pressed down on my wrist with all his weight. My elbow was at the closest edge of the block and I couldn't bend my arm. I couldn't back up, either, since Janne, who felt like he weighed a hundred kilos, was ramming me up against the block.

"Thieves get their hands cut off so they can't steal anymore," Hiililuoma screamed. "Or vandalize walls. Or destroy decent people's property."

I tried to wriggle my hand out of Hiililuoma's grasp, but it was like a vise. I couldn't pull back a single centimeter. Janne was pressing into my back like a collapsed wall.

"What the fuck did you do?" Hiililuoma asked, the axe dropping in an arc of light.

Lightning struck one of the outdoor lights a few meters away, and the lamp shattered with a pop, shooting out sparks and shards of glass. It startled Janne and his weight eased off. I lunged backward. The back of my head bumped into Janne's chin.

Hiililuoma didn't loosen his grip.

He should have.

Just as the axe was landing I managed to yank my arm free from the block, and Hiililuoma's arm slid down the wet block as I pushed myself away. He chopped his own wrist, severing his ulna and his radius and the sinews of his forearm. The ends of his bones gleamed white in the rain. I've never heard a sound like the one he made.

At the same instant, a dark figure rushed at me. The other giant schnauzer was loose. It rushed past, and I fell back. I somehow struggled to my feet. Hiililuoma leapt out in front of me. He still held the axe in his right hand, and he was swinging it wildly. I feinted and slipped, stumbling forward a couple of steps. The creature I had mistaken for the giant schnauzer was rolling around on the ground with Janne. It was Vorkuta!

I pulled at Janne's coat and hair, and as we grappled his coat came free. I once again fell down on the grass. Before I could get up Hiililuoma collapsed on me, digging his knees into my chest. He brought the axe down. I was too close and the blade sank into the lawn above my scalp. But the handle bashed my already-mangled nose. Hiililuoma changed tack and started pressing the handle crosswise against my throat. Red spots danced in front of my eyes.

My spasming fingers struck on some small, hard object. I managed to dig a car key out of the pocket of Janne's coat. I braced the butt of the key against my palm and drove the tip through Hiililuoma's cheek. The second stab caught him in the eye. He howled and let go of my throat. I rolled to the side, able to breathe again.

Janne was straddling Vorkuta, relentlessly punching his face. My hands fumbled for a log, and I cracked it against Janne's head. It knocked him out cold, and I helped the bleeding Vorkuta up from the lawn.

As we ran off into the darkness a car pulled up at the far end of the grounds. In its headlights I saw a silhouette hacking the air to bits with an axe.

BLACK WATER

Vorkuta led me through the spruces to the mouth of the bunker. I protested; I thought we should keep moving. Vorkuta reminded me that a car had just pulled into Paradise, which meant search-party reinforcements. On the road, we'd get caught; in the stormy woods we'd get lost if we were lucky and end up dead under a tree if we weren't.

"Metro, you look like a zombie," he said. "You're not going to make it far in that condition, and neither am I."

I didn't have the energy to argue so I scrambled under the decaying tree and plunged into the bunker we had opened a few hours earlier. I was soaking wet and shivering. I wanted to leave the iron door ajar. I dreaded the thought of ending up in a place that didn't have an escape route.

We waited silently at the bunker's mouth. Vorkuta pressed up against me when his teeth started chattering.

A beam of light flashed past in the rain-soaked spruces. And another.

"We need to go deeper," Vorkuta said.

We retreated to the doors deeper in the tunnel.

"We can't go back to that cellar."

"Maybe they won't come in here."

We leaned against the freezing wall for a second and then retraced our steps to the bunker's entrance.

The thunder rumbled, accompanied by a growl almost as deep.

"Shit," I said.

"What?"

"That second giant schnauzer. Josie."

The beams of light dancing in the darkness were much closer now; there were at least four of them. Once again, we retreated to the two interior doors. We both stared at the one we hadn't opened yet, the one on the left.

Vorkuta shook his head. "It leads into the sea."

"Baron said there's air at the end."

"After all this do you trust anything he told us?"

"What I'm not going to do is end up back in their clutches."

Vorkuta grabbed my arm. I wrenched free when the first beam of light penetrated the bunker. I snatched Vorkuta's bolt cutters and snapped off the rusty metal around the old padlock. I opened the squealing door just wide enough for me to slip through. Vorkuta followed and pulled the door nearly shut behind him. The tunnel started to descend and before long we were wading through thigh-deep water. I tasted it; it had a salty tang. We could hear voices echoing in the bunker behind us. I tried not to splash as I walked.

After about ten meters the tunnel dropped so steeply that I was up to my neck in black water that was lapping at the roof; the surface shivered under my heavy breathing.

"Are you sure?" Vorkuta asked.

I heard the hollow woof of a dog in the bunker. I nodded and slid in. I still had my headlamp on; the light reflected back from particles swirling in the dark water. Visibility was lousy; my arm dimmed at the elbow and my fingers didn't even exist.

At first I kicked ferociously, but I was afraid of using up too much oxygen, so I forced myself to calmly pull forward.

A glittering fish with black scales swam past.

I banged my head; it had taken far too many blows today. An iron bar was sticking down from the roof of the tunnel. My unintentional headbutt caused a rain of rust to shiver down, making the water murkier. I should have been counting how many times I'd kicked. It felt like I had already gone fifty meters; Baron had mentioned twenty.

I ran out of breath.

I felt the ceiling overhead as I desperately kicked forward. My head was rubbing rough concrete.

It was too late to go back now.

The light was more disorienting than helpful. It bounced through the coal-black water. The pressure in my ears was intensifying. I was going deeper and deeper.

I had to breathe.

Ten more seconds.

I can do this, goddammit.

My ears were killing me.

I furiously dragged myself forward. One second, two seconds, three, four, five. My lungs were burning; the strength had drained out of my legs. This is what Smew felt like when his Dad tossed him in the lake so he'd learn how to swim. Smew was afraid of water for the rest of his brief existence.

Ten. I had to inhale now, water or no.

Eleven, twelve.

At thirteen, my head no longer scraped the ceiling. I turned my face up.

I breathed. There was about twenty centimeters between the surface of the water and the ceiling overhead. I raised the hand holding the headlamp out of the water and aimed the light around. I was in a small chamber. There seemed to be a bigger gap right in the middle, not quite half a meter.

Even though the air had grown stale over the decades, to my lungs it felt fresher than a winter breeze.

My feet couldn't touch the bottom. My legs were getting tired fast as I treaded water to keep from sinking. A couple of bits of metal were sticking out of the walls; I paddled over to one and held on for a second.

I dove down and explored all the walls. My lungs emptied more quickly than they had a moment ago. I returned to the surface; my breath was rasping.

I turned off the headlamp; I needed to save the light.

I started silently counting to a hundred; at sixty-two, there was a splash inside the chamber.

I turned on my headlamp. Vorkuta was coming from the other end of the cavern.

"There's a bar over here," I said. "Come hold on to it."

"Fuck, they're all in the bunker," he huffed, once his breath grew steadier.

"All? How many is all?"

"Three flashlights, at least. And a dog."

"Did they notice you?"

"I don't think so."

"There's nowhere to go from here. It's a dead end. I dove down and checked. There's only one hole big enough to swim through. The one we came from."

"OK."

"Is your clock working?" I asked.

Vorkuta pulled out his alarm clock. A drop of water had crept under the glass. The second hand fought against the droplet, but it couldn't pop through the surface tension. We were living in an eternal three minutes to midnight.

The cold crept into my limbs. I slipped out into the middle of the chamber now and again to tread water, but my legs got tired before they had a chance to warm up. They were numb from the knees down.

"Tell me about Orgosolo," I said, teeth chattering. "What happened after you and Alyosha went into that barn? The one where they'd been keeping skunks."

In a shivering voice, Vorkuta told me that a knock at the door had woken them at dawn. When he opened it, he found two big cups of coffee, along with a hunk of cheese and half a loaf of bread. He tried to thank the neighbors but they still wouldn't open the door. He and Alyosha headed out to wander the village and ended up at a home with a wall overlooking a ravine; a group of men were busy painting it. It turned out the group consisted of three generations: grandfathers and their sons and grandsons.

I interrupted him. "What about girls?"

"The girls paint, too, but these were men," Vorkuta said, floating there in the watery darkness.

The blackness was so visceral I could feel it on my skin. It was more bone chilling than the water.

"They were painting a mural of an Indian camp," Vorkuta continued. "Below, there was a valley like the one that opened up beyond the cliff. They were painting their homes into teepees and their village into an Indian camp. At the corner, an old man in a beret was painting a portrait of himself as an old chief gazing down across the valley. His grandson painted a speech bubble over the chief's head: *Even if you live to be a hundred years, you cannot take the riches of this earth with you.* Alyosha and I sat down and watched for hours as the boys and men from the village created their communal piece. Finally they stopped and started walking down the lane, covered in paint. The oldest man stopped by where we were sitting and gestured for us to follow him. We wound our way through the village, following the scent of food. We ended up at a small square, where almost the entire village had gathered. In the heart of the village there was a fire pit; an entire wild boar was being spit-roasted. Like in the final scene of every *Asterix* comic book, where the bard is tied to a tree while everyone else chows down on roasted boar."

"You guys walked into a comic book," I said, my tongue stiff from the cold.

"It wasn't a comic book, it was real," Vorkuta said. "Writer heaven. Paradise for graffiti artists. That's where we're going to end up once we freeze to death and drown in this fucking grave. Alyosha is already waiting for me there."

After dinner and countless glasses of moonshine, Vorkuta and Alyosha were led back to the house where they had knocked at the door. This time, instead of being sent out to the barn, they were shown upstairs to a room with beds.

They lived in the Sardinian village for two months, painting with the villagers, eating at a different home every night, making the rounds as honored guests. They could paint graffiti and murals to their hearts' content. The villagers had a deal with anarchists and journalists, which meant that in addition to their quarry, the SUV-driving hunters with shotguns slung across their backs brought cans of latex and spray paint from their excursions. The villagers never ran out of painting supplies.

"Why did you leave?" I asked.

"They were trying to marry us off to local girls. Things got a little tricky," Vorkuta said. "And I started having a bad conscience. There was no way life could be that pleasurable. As if someone had given us a love potion and enchanted us so we'd never leave. If we'd stayed there even a week longer we never would have escaped. We'd have stayed spellbound in Orgosolo. Hell, until we died. It was like a trip that was too good. One night we snuck into the barn and pushed the motorcycle down the village road. I let it coast for a long time before I dared start it. When we looked up from down below the lights in the village were coming on one by one. It looked like part of the starry sky. Someone up above was calling out our names longingly."

"It won't be long before we're there," I shivered.

I could barely move my lips; my tongue wouldn't twist properly in my mouth. I sounded even drunker than Vorkuta and his muttered gibberish.

"No, it won't," Vorkuta said.

There was a splash in the darkness, then another.

"Is that you?" I said.

"No. I'm not moving."

I turned on my headlamp. In the middle of the chamber I saw the big, black head of the giant schnauzer turning this way and that. It was treading water and eyeing us, teeth bared.

Josie picked me and started swimming over. I slid past her to the other side of the chamber, where Vorkuta was waiting. I pulled the bolt cutters out of his backpack. The giant schnauzer tried to grab hold of the bar jutting out from the wall, then she turned around and headed for me again.

"If those jaws get hold of one of our arms or legs it's fucking *do svidanya*," Vorkuta said.

He managed to slip past the snap of the hound's jaws and headed to the far side of the chamber. I stayed where I was and whacked the approaching snout with the bolt cutters as hard as I could. The dog howled and started splashing more ferociously than before. I dove below her flailing legs to the other side of the chamber. She turned and headed for me again.

"Stop, already," I begged.

But she didn't. I bashed Josie in the nose again, dove back through the black water to the other wall of the chamber, and hung from the bar. This went on over a dozen times. The giant schnauzer would lunge, I'd smack her with the bolt cutters and swim to the far side of the cavern. One time she managed to catch the collar of my jacket and ripped my coat in half with a single jerk of her head. The water around Josie was turning red. Her growls dwindled to pants and plaintive whimpers.

"It can't do anything to us anymore," Vorkuta said, almost thankfully.

"She sure can," I panted. "She'll grab hold of us and drag us down to the bottom with the last of her fucking strength."

I clobbered Josie one more time. She yelped and suddenly tried to wag her tail. *Come on, we're friends, aren't we?*

"I have a hard time believing you," I said.

Eventually the giant schnauzer's splashing slowed; she stopped turning around to pursue us. We listened to the rattle as she tried to breathe through her bloody, broken mouth and nose. I had smashed some of her teeth, and she was choking on her own blood.

Josie finally sank below the surface. I turned off my headlamp so Vorkuta wouldn't see my tears.

THE ONLY REAL ROAD

Vorkuta helped me stay afloat as I sprayed METRO and VORKUTA on the chamber's ceiling, and next to that, RUST, ALYOSHA, and SMEW. Then I painted an ice-skating rat. My hand was shaking so badly that the fur turned out fuzzier than I meant it to.

"It's the new Ice Cave," I said, my teeth chattering.

Maybe some cave diver would find these marks on the ceiling ten thousand years from now, when our era was considered a barbarian Stone Age during which people hated and killed each other, even though they claimed to be acting out of love and a sense of responsibility. For the common good.

We counted together to a thousand and again a second time, and we started on a third time. We kept getting mixed up, and by the end our tongues were so numb that counting anymore was pointless, and we left the chamber.

I sank down into the water and aimed for the black hole at the bottom that I had emerged from. Months ago, it felt like.

At the end of my dive, a faint light gleamed up ahead. I thought it was a flashlight beam, but I couldn't help thrusting my head to the surface. I was dying for air.

It took me only a moment to realize the light was the glow of sunrise. The world was eerily still. At this time of summer, even the birds weren't singing.

I clambered out of the water. My legs were so stiff that they wouldn't bend properly at the knees.

I waited for Vorkuta. He still had the cutters. Once he was out of the water we fumbled our way through the winding passage and into the bunker proper. No one was there. The light was brighter now, a naked glare unsoftened by the green of the spruces. It felt like a dentist's drill.

I peered out the door of the bunker. The sun was still low, shining straight into my eyes from between the trunks. Most of it still lay buried in the moss. I could make out a sliver of bruise-blue sky between the crowns of the trees.

A lone bird cried off in the distance. Raindrops plopped into a pool from the branches of a spruce.

We walked through the woods, making for the rising sun. Mosquitoes joined us; their whining was a relief, like a friendly whisper in my ear.

The storm had gusted through, hoeing up pieces of the forest. Dozens of fallen and splintered trunks painted pale stripes amid the dusky spruces. Some that had been overturned at the roots clung by their branches to the evergreens that still stood. Their leaning trunks creaked overhead as we walked beneath them.

We arrived at a narrow dirt road where the sun was shining directly in front of us. The entire surface of the road was covered in countless needles that had been knocked from their branches. They glowed in the sun, gold and green.

Trees had crashed down across this golden path; one fat birch had cracked in half at a height of five meters. The broken crown was still attached to the trunk by the bark and a few slivers of wood; it formed a creaking black-and-white gate we passed through.

"I'm freezing. The sun's not warming me up," I said.

"Of course you're freezing; you're an Ice Rat," Vorkuta said.

The ferocious currents of the storm had ravaged the grounds of Janus's dacha yesterday, but the sky showed no sign of it; if it weren't for the tangle of fallen trees and the fat carpet of needles blanketing the surface of the road, you'd have never known. The sun was painting the sky a more vivid blue with every second that passed.

"Shouldn't we head west so we don't end up in Russia?" Vorkuta asked.

"West is where that goddamn Paradise is. Between us and Kotka."

We stepped off the road and headed back into the brush; we didn't want to run into any road-clearing crews. After a sweaty trudge through the spruces, we stopped in a spot where the Ice Age had rolled up a boulder the size of a house, with a line of five smaller ones next to it.

"Rock babies," Vorkuta said. "They're following their mama like ducklings."

I sat down on one of the small boulders and carefully rolled down my soaking trousers. My thigh was covered in vertical contusions; two bloody arcs glared back at me from the bruised skin, which flapped loose at one end.

"You need to get that leg of yours to a doctor," Vorkuta said. "You don't want the bite to get infected." He slipped out of his wet shirt, tore off the sleeves, and used them to bind the wound. "There's no way I'm ever going to get that clean."

We walked through forest for so long that the sun had time to rise and spin over to our right, above the sea that occasionally shimmered between the trunks. Trees smacked down by the storm hindered our progress. It felt like we were picking our way through a giant's obstacle course. My legs were stiff from the kicking and the beating and the biting; when one of my knees hit the ground, a stinging pain shot through my whole leg.

We followed the densest spruce-woods and thickets. The ferns reached up to my neck, and as we plunged through the jungle of greenery we sent dozens of dragonflies and butterflies flitting into the air. The ferns came to a sudden end at an inlet lush with reeds. A man with a beard sat at the shore, untangling his nets. It was too late to retreat. I said hello; he grunted.

"Where you headed?" he asked.

"Kotka."

"Wrong direction," he said.

"The road's blocked."

"The only real road is the sea," the old fellow growled.

The sun was finally warming me up a little so I leaned back, closed my eyes, and let the red glow behind my eyelids permeate my whole head. My ears were buzzing with the question of whether I had left any traces at Janus's manor. I had worn gloves while I was painting, same with when I handled the jug of acid. There was nothing in my backpack that would identify me, and Vorkuta still had his own pack. The rain would have washed anything outside into oblivion. The security cameras had been blacked out.

I wasn't so worried about the police; I doubted the story would make it to them. It was more likely that the windows would be washed and that Rannikko's death by dog and Hiililuoma's self-amputation would be recorded as little more than accidents. The thunderstorm had driven the dog crazy; Hiililuoma's axe had slipped in the rain.

I was most worried about Janus, Pavel Putikov, a man I had never seen. His goons in Berlin had whacked Smew and Alyosha and Dad, just for being in the wrong place at the wrong time. Janus had the ability and the resources to shape people and the world according to his wishes with either a carrot or a stick, by hiring the functionaries of violence to hunt down complications such as myself who spoiled his views. My vengeance paled in comparison to their methods.

Although revenge could momentarily serve as the most powerful of engines, it had a tendency to run out of fuel if you were wet and cold despite the summer sunshine. I doubted anything could make the lust for power dwindle.

"We need to spilt up," Vorkuta said through the drone of the flies, as if he had been thinking the same thing about Janus. "If we're together it'll be easier for them to catch us."

"Doesn't your friend speak Finnish?" the fisherman asked.

"No."

"I'll be damned. What does he speak then? Nubian?"

"English."

"All of them languages are the same. No use for any of 'em. Except Finnish."

"Well, I speak Finnish. Can you take us to Kotka?" I asked. "By boat?"

"How much are you willing to pay?"

Vorkuta and I dug through our pockets and Vorkuta's backpack. We came up with two wrinkled five-euro bills.

"I don't have any use for your money. What I want is them cutters."

The fisherman had noticed Vorkuta's bolt cutters. We accepted the offer. He grumbled at his nets a bit longer, then he waved us over to his wooden boat.

"Kotka, you said?"

"Lehmäsaari Island."

I flattened myself against the waterlogged bottom of the boat; the morning sun had already warmed the puddle there. A tern was fishing nearby; it missed several times but always rose again to find an underwater victim, hovering like a helicopter between strikes.

The shoreline was dotted with storm-savaged trees. Vorkuta and I stayed low the whole time, below the sides of the boat. Janus's Paradise was out there somewhere in the middle of the flattened forest. Even though the sky was clear, the choppy sea still rolled in long swells, and cradled in the boat's rocking we fought against sleep. My foot throbbed. I imagined how the skin around the dog bite would turn black, and the blackness would eventually devour me.

I started when the boat rocked in the opposite direction.

"I'm not asleep!" I cried.

"It was hard to hear the engine for all your snoring," our pilot said, and grunted.

We were entering the narrow strait where the biggest maritime battle in Northern Europe had taken place. The navies of Sweden and Russia had met between Lehmäsaari Island and the mainland; almost five hundred vessels had fired on each other at close range. The sea bottom was thick with bits of sunken vessels, rusted cannons, loose limbs, shattered skulls, and graceful cockades admired by no one but perches and eels these days. Eight thousand skeletons lay there at the bottom.

Old Man Beard killed the motor at the site of the battle. "Time to pay up," he growled.

Vorkuta handed over the cutters. Old Man Beard examined them for a moment and then dropped them into the water.

"There's still some room at the bottom."

He drove us to the island's long sandy beach and helped me and my bad legs climb over the side.

"Folks came around asking for you this morning," he said. "Looking for a black girl and a pale feller."

"Police?"

"Didn't speak proper Finnish," said Old Man Beard, shaking his head. "Couldn't understand what they were saying. I'm just a fisherman. Looked angry. Don't reckon it'll be long before they're headed this way, too."

I gave him a hug. He cleared his throat, asked me to shove the boat out of the shallows so the motor wouldn't catch on the bottom.

I stood there until the boat disappeared behind Kukouri, the little island with the fortress on it. We warily waded ashore through the knee-deep water, like explorers approaching an unmapped island, wary of spear-brandishing natives and hungry tigers lurking in the bushes.

The tent was still there. No one had touched Vorkuta's pinecone welcome or the four pairs of men's swimming trunks hanging from the line.

I felt like lying down and sleeping, just sleeping, for thousands and thousands of years.

We started taking down the tent.

BANKSY

A nightingale sang alluringly from the kitchen table. I hesitated for a moment before picking up Mom's cell phone and cutting off the nightingale ring.

"Mademoiselle Miranda, how may I help you?" I pronounced the r the gravelly way I imagined French people did.

The caller was a woman with an anemic voice who wanted to hear about her future. I told her that I sensed she was an artistic and gifted individual whose current circumstances blocked her from making the most of her strengths. When it came out that she was single, I promised her not only a new job, but a good man, two beautiful children, a happily-ever-after, and a pet in the form of a faithful puppy. A little dog that would never bite anyone ever. This was what my cards said. The woman should pay attention to people wearing green for the following week. Not the dark green appearing, for instance, on the uniforms of some security companies, but the tender green of a budding birch tree or a fresh-cheeked apple. A person wearing a shirt or shorts in that hue would bring change. New life springs forth!

I wished the woman a future of happy days and cloudless skies. Then I ended the call.

I looked in the mirror to see how long my nose had grown from all the fibbing.

I glanced at the timer to check how long the call had lasted: three and a half minutes. Mom would have stretched it out for another five minutes, at a rate of five euros and ninety-nine cents a minute.

In under a year, Mom had been forced to lower her rates for her over-the-phone fortune-telling by two euros a minute. I had suggested she might want to switch professions again soon to, say, selling tips on long-odds bets. They had a better chance of coming true than her predictions. Mom claimed that the decrease in demand for her services had nothing to do with the quality of her clairvoyance. It was all because of the recession and the spineless government that didn't support honest entrepreneurs. In addition—and Mom was emphatic about this—fortune-telling was infinitely more emotionally rewarding than the phone-sex work she used to do.

Mom considered herself one of the most hardworking entrepreneurs in Karhuvuori. My view was that she worked really hard at collecting all kinds of benefits and subsidies from the welfare office while hiding her fortune-telling income from the tax office.

Whenever the phone rang, Mom turned into Mademoiselle Miranda, a psychic who promised people romantic, debt-free futures, unexpected inheritances, sudden wealth, and surprising twists in their grim, gray lives. As far as her clients were concerned, she read these amazing things from tarot cards. I had never seen her use so much as a postcard in her fortune-telling, let alone tarot cards; she'd pop off the same things to everyone who called, just in a different order.

I had promised to step in for Mom this afternoon and take her calls; she had gone out to get some exercise.

I sighed and looked out the kitchen window.

The grounds of the nearby apartment buildings were at their lushest in August; the tall grass mercifully concealed the broken bottles and the junkies. The parking lot was empty. It was Saturday and any and all neighbors capable of stumbling out of their apartments had grabbed a boat and made for the islands. No self-respecting Kotka resident ever goes inland when they have time off; they head for the water and the horizon. The sea is their trip abroad.

A group of boys was sitting at the edge of the forest. The one with the dreads had a bucket upside down in front of him, and he was drumming the bottom of it with two sticks. And so a band is born.

The decor in Mom's apartment had changed since the previous fall, when I had last paid her a visit. It had been my birthday back then, and everything had glowed a penetrating orange, from the curtains to Mom's outfit and hair. My birthday cake had been decorated with tangerine slices, and earrings like little oranges had dangled from Mom's ears. She had given me the ugliest homemade batik tablecloth in a print that reminded me of amoebas. Orange, of course. *The sun, my dear, life and joy,* Mom had said. *Orange is a ray of sunlight that opens you up to opportunities.*

The orange phase had been preceded by a turquoise one.

Now orange had vanished completely from the apartment. The curtains had switched to bright apple green, as had the tablecloth and the pillowcases and Mom's cell phone cover.

I'd been staying with her for three days now, and she had worn an apple-green top every single day. Her earrings were also a delicate green. A big poster had appeared on the wall of—wouldn't you know—a basket of Granny Smith apples.

"Isn't it the season of orange anymore?" I had asked Mom the day before, as she painted her toenails lettuce green. "Aren't we children of the sun, like last time I was here?"

She had said that now was the time for growth, both spiritual and physical. *Without sprouts there are no plants, my dear. Without plants there is no oxygen. Without oxygen neither you, Maria, nor I can breathe and flourish. Change starts from the hue of leaves. The buds of the birch, pea shoots. Chlorophyll.*

Mom hadn't stopped babbling, and I had moved from the couch to the beanbag and from the beanbag to the floor, where I pulled a blanket over my head. I couldn't get comfortable. When I was a kid I had all kinds of favorite spots at home where I'd curl up and feel safe.

Earlier in the summer, Mom had gone to the doctor for the first time in years and had been encouraged to get out and get more exercise. That's supposedly what she was doing now. As far as I could tell this consisted of smoking out in front of the little local shopping center, between the BarBaari pub and the convenience store. After seeing the doctor, Mom had also decided to adopt a vegan diet. In the fridge, above the heads of lettuce and bunches of carrots, there were a few packs of hot dogs and a salami. Mom called it her vegan first-aid kit. In case she started feeling weak.

I hadn't told her anything about what happened to Dad. Or to little Samuel, whom I had abandoned in Berlin. Or that I had spent the last few months in Berlin. After Mom's persistent inquiries, I lied and said I'd spent the summer in Kouvola. There's a busy railway station with a billiard club in the basement. You can grab a train when you get tired of the fuzzy-dice douchebags driving back and forth, cruising for pussy. Mom thought I was still working at a shoe store in Kouvola and that I was on my summer vacation.

"Do you have a boyfriend there?" she had asked.

"Nope."

"Don't you think it's time to get one?"

The nightingale twittered. I introduced myself as Mademoiselle Miranda. Another female caller. This one had a low smoker's voice. She spoke quickly, jabbering something about being at a seminar and calling during a break. Over her lifetime, she had been sent to dozens of these development seminars by her employers and in all the time she had spent at them she hadn't improved her professional skills or self-esteem. As a matter of fact, the only thing that had shot up was her blood pressure.

I told her that the tarot cards urged her to either give notice or start a career as a seminar speaker. She had a brilliant future ahead of her no matter which one she chose.

I turned on Mom's computer and logged into an e-mail account registered under a name that only one person in the world knew. I chewed my lip until it bled. The message I had been waiting for had finally arrived.

I clicked on the attachment, and a video clip popped up on the screen, showing a drawbridge going up, revealing a dick dozens of meters tall. It rose till it was pointing across the Neva River, toward the headquarters of the Russian security police.

Vorkuta had made it to safety.

I reclined on the rug. My eyes grew wet, even though they were closed.

I hadn't heard from Vorkuta in three days. The last time I saw him, during the boat ride from the island to the mainland, he had knocked together a four-minute video from the material he had shot at Janus's. The clip began with the text advertising the auction: FIRST BANKSY MURAL WITH A CERTIFICATE OF AUTHENTICITY. After that came SOLD FOR 2.2 MILLION EUROS, followed by huge pulsing exclamation points. Then it showed footage of the Pest Control certificate and *Ice Rat*, both of which had been shot in Janus's gallery the night of the thunderstorm. Next you saw me, face hidden by my shemagh, meticulously destroying *Ice Rat* with acid before burning the certificate of authenticity.

The final text read: WHAT YOU ACQUIRE BY UNJUST MEANS, JUSTICE WILL TAKE FROM YOU. HI JANUS!!! FUCK YOU!!! THE ICE RATS. THANK YOU.

The clip ended with words that remained on-screen: THE DESTRUCTION OF BANKSY'S ICE RAT IS DEDICATED TO THE MEMORIES OF ALYOSHA, SMEW, AND SAMUEL.

Over the past three days, the video had spread across graffiti-themed sites and YouTube like wildfire through dry grass. It had racked up almost four million views.

I turned off the computer and walked over to the window. A black Mercedes had pulled into the parking lot of the building next door. This was the first time it had been there. I had made a note of the neighbors' cars during my stay at Mom's. This wasn't one of them.

Maybe it was someone's aunty coming to visit.

Maybe not.

It was time for me to scram.

Mom's phone rang; I didn't answer.

I went into the bedroom and opened up Mom's drawers. Her closet was full of hair-care products; one of the businesses that had attracted Mom's attention during recent years was pyramid schemes. She had committed to selling thousands of bottles of shampoo and eventually sold two, including the one I bought under duress. She had enough shampoo to last her until 2134.

I rummaged through Mom's underwear drawer. She kept her money at the bottom. I had known about this cache for years, but I hadn't tapped it until now. I found over fifteen hundred euros in a pair of bunched-up pantyhose. I left her a couple hundred and took the rest.

I glanced out the window; the black Mercedes was still in the parking lot. The sun was reflecting off its windshield; I could see someone at the wheel.

I packed my bag. I wrote the word *sorry* on a piece of paper and left it on the kitchen table. As an afterthought, I scribbled *M.*

The nightingale warbled again; it was a good day for Mom. I was starting to see how you could get hooked on this psychic gig. You just kicked back on the couch and painted your toenails, and people paid you to prattle away. Maybe Mom should start being a seminar speaker; there was no more shit coming out of her mouth than anyone else's.

I stepped back into the kitchen and snagged the phone.

"Mademoiselle Miranda, how may I help you?"

"Metro."

My brain felt like it had been emptied.

"Mademoiselle Miranda on the line, how may I help you?"

"Cheers, Metro," said the voice at the other end of the line. "How's it going?"

"You must have the wrong number," I answered, shivers running down my neck.

"Thanks for giving my work a proper funeral," the voice continued.

A jolt ran through me like an electric shock. The phone dropped to the floor, knocking the cover off. I fumbled for the phone and picked it up.

"Banksy?"

"Metro," the voice answered calmly.

Banksy was famous for being invisible. He never appeared in public, even at his own shows, and the handful of people who knew his real identity were loyal to the death. You couldn't reach him; there was no way of contacting him. He was a ghost.

"So you saw the video?"

"It's pretty hard to miss. You've done an incredible job spreading it online."

"Sorry," I said. "It was an amazing piece."

"In the wrong hands," the voice answered. "The mural you painted in Pripyat is also sweet. Great piece."

"You saw that?"

"In the flesh. I also liked the birch tree growing through the floor."

"How did you find me?" I asked. "This is my mom's work number."

"If I were you, I'd start thinking about my next step," the voice answered. "If I can find you, other people can, too."

Pause.

"And it won't be long before they do."

ABOUT THE AUTHOR

Photo © 2014 Havu Järvelä

Jari Järvelä has written novels, short stories, and essays, as well as plays for the stage and radio. He currently resides in Kotka, Finland, living between the ocean and a river. Naples and Marseille are his favorite cities because nothing works in them but everything works out, giving their citizens reasons to believe in miracles. His hobbies include karate, wines, and history. He is also passionate about punk music and fifteenth-century paintings, both of which indulge frenzied creation.

ABOUT THE TRANSLATOR

Photo © 2015 Lisa Loop

Kristian London has translated numerous Finnish-language plays and novels, including Petri Tamminen's *Crime Novel* and Harri Nykänen's *Nights of Awe*, a WLT Notable Translation of 2012. A native of the Pacific Northwest, he currently divides his time between Seattle and Helsinki.